THE
JIMSONWEED
FILE

To Mike & Rebecca

Tony Im

THE
JIMSONWEED
FILE

TONY IRONS

PISCATAQUA
PRESS

The Jimsonweed File

Copyright 2019 by Tony Irons

The Jimsonweed File is a work of fiction, except as modified by the Author's Note at the end of the book. The characters and plot are pure invention and not intended to represent either biography or an historical record. Except for review purposes, no part of this book may be used or reproduced in any manner without written permission. For more information please contact info@piscataquapress.com

ISBN: 978-1-950381-25-8

Printed in the United States

Published by
RiverRun Select, and imprint of
Piscataqua Press
32 Daniel St.
Portsmouth, NH 03801

for

Randy, Rusty

Moses and Zackary

my boys

Also by Tony Irons

Hoover's Children

Dengman Gap

*A Ragged Saint**

*soon to be a motion picture

"Buddy our boy can become president of the USA and we can engineer it. I will get all of Putin's team to buy in on this."

Felix Slater
Russian born real estate developer
Message to Michael Cohen, childhood friend

1

MY NAME IS TOBIAS STARKEY. I am a newsman, an investigative reporter. I ask questions, often difficult or uncomfortable questions. I research things and dig up documents, ask more questions of people who really don't want to talk to me. I spend my days in public libraries reading old newspaper stories, in county Halls of Records, Tax Assessors' offices, county jails, police stations, the courts—local, state and federal—the lobbies of corporations (because I never get past the lobby) and stalking the hallways outside the private sanctums of elected officials. I search the Internet, surfing from one site to another, bringing up obscure academic treatises, conspiracy theories, blogs and government postings.

Some of what I get is from the bars where all these people go after the time clock rings five. There they gather for drinks and chatter and I listen, engage with equanimity, always watching gestures, body language, laughter, associations, seeing who knows what and I write it all down later in my apartment or hotel room. They know who I am and what I'm doing, so anything they say loud enough for me to hear is intended to reach my ears. Some, I would even call my friends. Then I pull it all together in a story for my editor's consideration. Occasionally, I sniff out a story good enough to hoist myself up a rung on the newsbeat ladder, but each time I do, some other hungry reporter, with a few more story-notches in his belt, slides in and scoops it. I go back to my cubicle and follow more puny

1

leads. I'm new at this, not tough enough yet, but when Trump won the election it was all hands on deck, as many eyes and ears as could be mustered to handle all the strange and dangerous news. The news came like machine-gun staccato out of the White House, mostly from the president himself, all designed to distract a free press from any rational research or analysis.

I have heard stories of people taking a reporter aside, tugging at a sleeve or cupping the crook of an arm and pulling him or her into a corridor by the bathrooms. Or just whispering, asking to meet in some unlit or remote place to give information about a dark thing that shouldn't be overheard and otherwise would never be found. Like Deep Throat. That happens to the most seasoned, the most hardened reporters, like Woodward and Bernstein, the kind of reporters that a deep throat would trust never to blow their cover. Not guys like me. But that is exactly what happened with Mr. Hamilton—my rifle safety and hunting instructor—my childhood mentor—the man who got me this job at the *Boston Globe*.

It was eight o'clock at night on Wednesday, November 8, 2017. I was 24 years old. I was tired, worn-out, my mind beginning to drift from voice to voice, face to face, unable to pair them together to get one talking head. I was getting ready to leave the local dive two blocks from City Hall when the bartender handed me the phone.

"It's for you." That was odd—nobody knew I was there.

It was a woman's voice.

"Go to the Sir John Motel tomorrow evening at 5:30. Mr. Hamilton has a message for you." A click and the line went dead.

The Sir John Motel is, by any human measure, a revolting place. Clearly, no health inspector had ever been there or the whole building would have been bulldozed that very day. It sits on the northern edge of a parking lot serving The Pink Filly, a gentleman's club. There was a flashing red, white and blue marquee imploring all to see the *SUPER HOT, WET & WILD CANDI DUVALL TONIGHT AT 6:00.* The front of the motel building doesn't face the parking lot. What you see is the back—a wall of unpainted concrete blocks with six tiny windows too high to peek in. Nor is there any sign directing anyone to an office. It is left to the curious to conclude that the front must be on the other side. Which it is. It is in the shadows at the edge of a vast auto salvage yard. There is a narrow walkway and six rusting steel doors. One to each room. As I walked past the first door, a light went on at the end. Motion detector. The last door opened, and a man's voice said, "Yeah?" It sounded like a question.

"I'm here to meet someone."

"How long?"

"You mean how long will I be staying here? I don't know that yet."

"Then that'll be the maximum. Fifty bucks."

"What if I said just an hour?"

"That is the maximum."

"Oh." I decided to stand where I was, so he had to come to me and I could see him clearly, to document in my notes what he looked like, how he acted, like a good reporter would. I took fifty dollars from my wallet and held it out for him to take. He approached me slowly, carefully. I had been expecting a freak of some sort—a man of massive corpulence or a rat-faced person in lime green polyester. What came to me was a man in his thirties: shined boots, clean jeans, black V-neck tee-shirt, muscles with veins popping out. His face was square-jawed with a well-groomed three-day growth of beard, dark hair neatly trimmed and combed. On his forearm was a black tattoo of a frog skeleton. His hand extended and waited for me to put the money in his palm. He held out a key.

3

"Room three." He turned and walked back to the corner room. The back of his tee shirt said, *Built to Kick Ass.* That frog skeleton was the unofficial tattoo of a Navy Seal. I'd seen it on the internet.

There was a queen-size bed covered with a tattered and stained blue blanket and four pillows that were more like sofa cushions. An overstuffed chair leaked its overstuffing out of both arms. No bureau, no closet. On a desk in the corner was a TV screen sitting on a DVD player. The bathroom had once been painted pink, but all manner of human fluids and gasses had peeled most of the paint right off the concrete. I sat on a corner of the bed checking my watch, waiting. At five-thirty sharp there was a knock at the door.

She seemed to be from a corporate office of some sort. Her eyes were alive, dark brown behind black framed glasses. She wore a brown tailored woman's suit and jacket and black flats. Her hair was pulled to a bun, stuck through with a hair pin. She carried a large satchel. She locked the door and walked around the bed, her stare never leaving my face. She moved with a cleanliness of purpose, too much so I thought; her beauty—those eyes, wide mouth, and the sculpted form of her body—was hardened by an overwhelming absence of innocence.

"Are you Tobias Starkey?"

"Yes."

"Prove it."

I stood and handed her my driver's license and *Boston Globe* press credential.

"Okay." She handed them back. "Mr. Starkey, what type of gun is Mr. Hamilton's favorite deer hunting rifle?"

"Who are you? How did you know I was at that bar? It was you who called me, wasn't it?"

"Please, Mr. Starkey, just answer my question. What is Mr. Hamilton's favorite deer hunting rifle?"

"A Winchester Model 94."

She walked to the door, opened it and said, "Good-bye."

"No, no. Wait a minute, I was just testing you. The correct answer is a Remington Woodsmaster 742." I sat in the overstuffed chair and crossed my legs. The brown Naugahyde felt slippery.

"Don't test me. Just listen and watch. Okay?"

"Yes, but can I ask one question?"

"No."

"Who is this Navy Seal guy? Can't he get a better job somewhere where they need guys who can do all the shit he can do?"

She stood over me, pushed her glasses to the top of her head and leaned in close. Her breath was minty. She smelled like a citrus flower, maybe an orange blossom. Her lips, slightly parted, were a glossy rose. She was going to kiss me.

"Don't get cute. He's dangerous and…he's got a thing for guys like you," she whispered.

The notion of the man standing stork-like on one bent leg, then delivering a single blow to my throat wafted into an image of being bent over this chair, pants around my ankles, face implanted in the Naugahyde seat. It was at first 'distressing' but quickly moved to 'terrifying.' I jerked my elbows off the worn and ripped arms of the chair and jumped up, brushing off the detritus of stained stuffing.

She dumped the contents of her satchel on the bed. Thongs and panties, string bras, silky scarves, net stockings and a pair of stiletto heels. She looked up at me. I didn't say anything. She pulled a CD from a sleeve, put in the DVD machine, pushed the go button, sat on the bed and patted the space beside her. I sat.

A man in a topcoat was walking through a plaza. There was snow swirling in the air. A statue was off to the left; a robed woman holding branches on top of a very tall column. A modern building with a digital clock tower stood beyond. The clock said 8:21. The

5

sun was shining. It was morning. I was pretty sure it was Independence Square in Kiev, Ukraine. I had seen that square on the news when they were talking about Paul Manafort and the Russian-Ukrainian connection to the election. The man, hatless with a head of curly white hair, had his coat collar turned up. He greeted a woman with a hug. She was wearing a soviet-style fur hat, a thigh-length black leather jacket cinched tight at the waist and high black leather boots. The video, soundless, zoomed in on them until just their faces occupied the full screen. They were talking, hands held over their mouths. No lip reading possible. She was a stunning Slavic blonde. The screen went blank.

The next scene was at a swimming pool. The same curly-headed man was in a sweatshirt, sweatpants and flip-flops. Another man was in a suit with a bowtie. He was a small man with a black goatee and wire-rimmed glasses. They were sitting at a table by the pool, sipping drinks. Beyond a manicured shrub and flower garden was what looked like the back of a mansion. I could see two cars there. One, which looked like a new Mercedes, was pulled into a garage and the other, with a driver inside, was parked under the portico. The steering wheels were on the right-hand side. Somewhere in England. The camera panned around and the ocean was beyond, on the horizon. On the beach by the water's edge was a tall stone column, a tower with narrow windows going up the side.

Around the pool, lying in lounge chairs, were at least a dozen young women in bikinis. The camera once again enlarged to just the faces of the two men at the table. The curly-haired man held his chin in his hand, two fingers on his lips. No lip reading possible.

The third scene was through the glass window of a barber shop. It was filmed with a similar telephoto lens from some distance away.

The business sign on the window was in Russian. The spire and onion domes of St. Basil's Cathedral in Red Square could be seen beyond the barber shop building. The man in the chair getting his hair cut was the man from the plaza and the pool. It was a bit fuzzy through the window, but he was recognizable. The Slavic blonde from Kiev entered the barber shop with a man in military uniform—the gold waist belt, gold shoulder braids, a dozen medals and the black-brimmed hat of a high-ranking Russian military officer. Behind him was a short bald man in a baggy suit.

The screen went blank again and a voice came. I would know that voice anywhere. It was Mr. Hamilton. *Tobias, I have just found this document. It has been hidden for four years. That man in all three videos is the architect of current American national policy and the reason Trump was elected. He is Israeli and maybe British. Beyond that, I can find nothing. He is very dark, and his identity seems to be shielded by governments. Find him. The woman in the fur hat is, at the least, a very high-end hooker, if not a Russian agent. The man with the bowtie and goatee is a powerful banker, head of Sberbank. The officer is Sergey Shoygu, Russian Minister of Defense, the little man with him is Mayakovsky, GRU intelligence chief. I will soon have in my hands a second file which I believe will be explosive. It is being de-encrypted. I can't give this information to anyone—not the CIA, not the FBI, not the Justice Department. They all work for the president. If the media gets it first, it will be shredded as fake news. I have to hide it now. It is too dangerous. Don't let anyone know what you have seen and heard here. Remember the ten rules—especially number nine—when the bear comes after you, don't panic. Find my file. Don't let them cover it up. Godspeed, Tobias.*

Mr. Hamilton seemed to have been shaping my life to a certain purpose right from my childhood. I stared at the blank screen, dumfounded. Who *is* Mr. Hamilton? I thought I knew my friend. What does he mean—explosive, too dangerous?

She rose to eject the CD.

"Can you go back to the second scene?"

She looked at her watch, picked up the remote and ran it back to the second part. I got up close and could see the license plate on the rear of the car in the garage—AV16 PBR. I could also see that the girl sitting beside me in this fleabag-motel was one of the girls lounging by the pool. She ejected the disc.

"Can I have that?"

She flexed it, flexed it, flexed it, broke it in half and tossed the pieces in her satchel, took her jacket off, pulled the straight pin, shook her head, letting her hair cascade below her shoulders, lit a cigarette, kicked off her flats and began unbuttoning her blouse.

"Six o'clock. I have to go to work now, Mr. Starkey. Good-bye."

2

AFTER I GOT MY JOB AT THE *GLOBE*, I lived in Boston's Southie neighborhood. I found a two-room flat on the third floor of a three-story clapboard-sided apartment building. It had a bedroom roughly the size of a bed, a kitchen-dining-living area that sported an under-the-counter refrigerator, a two-burner stove top, a sink and an open space that could easily house two chairs and a small table. The bathroom had a feature I liked—a sink so close to the toilet that you had a place to put your coffee cup while sitting on the hopper. The room was wide enough to bend over to brush your teeth if you stood cock-eyed to the bowl, so your butt wouldn't bump the wall. Access to the shower stall was possible if, and only if, you took your clothes off in the living room. That wasn't a problem because the two windows in that room looked out on a magnificent blank brick wall five feet away. It was not possible for anyone to peer into my private space. I felt comfortable walking around naked. That was another plus that a little later turned into a big plus. I discovered that it was advisable to leave the windows closed because some scofflaw (I never could figure out who) used the five-foot-wide alley way between the two buildings as their personal dog kennel. But the biggest plus was the rent. To borrow a phrase from the real estate guy who showed it to me, the monthly damage was to die for—a thousand bucks. My mother had taken a yearlong sabbatical. The only thing she told me about it was she going off, with her boyfriend Gilbert, to the shores of the Arctic Ocean in the Northwest Territories, so I happily did this all by myself. Two grand for first and last. At the Salvation Army a block away, I gave them two hundred bucks for a couple each of plates, bowls, cups, knives, forks, spoons, frying pans, two chairs, a small table, a Modigliani print, sheets, blankets, a bed that could sleep two if one denizen was on the bottom, the other on the top and a light weight wicker sofa with polka-dot cushions. I lugged it all, piece by piece along the sidewalk and up the stairs.

Southie is a place where people hang together on the street and there's a pub on nearly every corner. Some of the apartment buildings, banks and police stations are brick, but most of the buildings are wood. In flush times, some of the clapboards and trim might have a coat of fresh paint, but most of the time, the apartment buildings are a damp gray, and the wood rail porches list to one side or the other. Wood is cheaper and faster than masonry, and there were trees in the forests of Ireland, so a rudimentary craft of carpentry survived in the families through the New World migration. Not the fine craftsmanship of the English or the Scandinavians, but enough to get a duplex built.

My office did not afford the same view as my apartment. It was a cubicle in the center of a big room surrounded by walls with doors in them, doors that lead to important people's offices. But then, I was new, the youngest except for the twenty-year-old secretary assigned to me and four other relative newcomers. She, Jasmine, was brash and sassy and somehow, at that young age, had mastered the skill of getting people on the phone to vomit up their whole life story while her fingers flew across her keyboard. She was going places—no question. The other guys she 'serviced' in our little clutch of cubicles made me swear a pact never to let on to any of the big-wigs how good she was. They'd snap her up in a minute.

After Trump was elected, the assignment I landed was given to me in a three-minute briefing by my new boss, Mr. Sam Borstien, in his corner office. I was to dig into the real estate holdings of a billionaire developer named Jimmy Frocinone, to investigate any connection between him and the Trump Organization. This was going to mean weeks spent searching records. I was cheaper than the consultants the paper often hired to do this kind of work. The upside was Mr. Borstien also said to talk to people involved on the construction side and folks who lived or worked in these high-rises.

A few weeks on the job and I had developed a serious lust for a girl who worked in the Registrar of Deeds office. The deeds were kept in massive leather-bound volumes arranged on the shelves by date going all the way back to the 1800s. Once I had figured out from the Tax Assessor's office the last date of a title transfer, I would go find Maggie to ask if she could spare a minute helping me find the deed. She had an angular face, brown eyes wide apart under arching eyebrows, Cherokee cheekbones and a narrowing jaw. Her mouth puckered when she was thinking and there was a dimple in the middle of her chin. She had freckles. Lots of them. I would be sitting in a wooden chair at a wooden desk with this leather tome open in front of me, pretending to be totally baffled. She would lean over my shoulder and flip the pages with a practiced precision, her very fine long hair falling across my neck. I could swear that the third or fourth time she helped me I could feel her breast brushing my shoulder.

After I put the last book back in its proper place, I asked her if she might consider having a drink with me after work. Her puckered mouth turned into a wide smile.

"Sure, but I get to pick the place. You don't mind tough and gritty, do you?"

Autumn in Boston. The slight breeze billowed out her hair and lace shawl as she walked beside me, holding my hand, pointing out all the local shops and what they sold and who owned them. She scowled as we walked past a check cashing place.

"Those guys make tons of money fleecing poor people who don't have any other way to get a nickel in this world." We walked past a liquor store and she asked me what my favorite drink was. I told her it was Jack Daniels straight up. I thought that sounded tough and kind of worldly-wise. After ten blocks or so we turned into a small street, more like an alley. There was a hand-painted wooden sign that pronounced, *Start Your Bender at The Old South Ender.*

"Uh, Maggie, are you sure of this?"

"Oh, yeah, quite sure. Most of the guys in here are off-duty cops, firemen and prosecutors from the District Attorney's office. It's the safest place in town." Her idea of safe and my idea of safe were leagues apart.

She patted my cheek, pushed the door open, and walked into a dark, noisy bar with a long bar counter and stool-type highchairs. A half dozen tables were along a side wall. Everything was very close and loud. The bar was full. Raucous. The Red Sox were on TVs all over the place. Maggie put her hand on my back and nudged me to the counter. The bartender, a tough looking red-faced guy in his fifties or so with a nose that took a serious turn to the left, pointed at two guys at the bar and commanded, "Hey you bums, get over to that table over there. Maggie's here."

We sat. The bartender leaned over the counter, his face not more than a foot in front of mine and said, "Whadda *you* want?"

Maggie said, "Daddy, don't be mean. This is Tobias. He's a friend of mine and he would very much like a double Jack Daniels straight up. Tobias, meet my father, Johnny James. And Daddy, I won't be home tonight."

It is known all over that it is far easier to find your way to a bar than it is to find your way home from a bar. Everybody knows it. Most people, after three double whiskeys and a couple of Guinness Stouts, can't even remember where they live, but for me that night, it was not a problem. Maggie remembered I had told her I lived across the street from the local library in Southie. When it was obvious we had to go, her daddy took out a short baseball bat from behind the counter, tapped it on the counter in front of me and said, "That's my baby girl. You watch yourself." He waved it around.

Maggie said, "Daddy, don't be mean." I stumbled out into the waiting embrace of a taxicab.

Here's where the plusses on my selection of an apartment really added up. Paid off big time. I brushed my teeth, washed my face and gargled, all sideways to the sink. Re-constituted, I came into my kitchen space. Maggie was standing in front of the window that looked out on nothing but brick.

She said, "Tobias, would you put on some music?" I pulled up Miles Davis *Sketches of Spain* on my phone and turned the volume up full. "You know what I've always wanted to do but never dared? I've always dreamed of standing in front of a big ol' window and doing this." She began to undulate to the syncopated beat, undoing her blouse one slow button at a time, letting it fall to the floor, then caressing free her bra, unzipping her skirt, rolling her hips until it too slithered down her legs. She slid out of her panties and eased them down to her feet, stepped clear of all her clothing, spread her arms and legs wide in front of the nowhere window, slow dancing to Davis, and shouted, "Yes!"

In the morning, she was on top. I don't recall how it all came about, but by the time we had to go to work, I had a girlfriend. An Irish firebrand, sweet as homemade sin.

This girl had an appetite. Voracious. She ate two complete orders of Mama D's breakfast special—fried eggs, bacon, Boston baked beans, wheat toast, coffee and orange juice. Two: that's four eggs, six slices of bacon, two helpings of beans, four slices of toast and both plates were shiny clean when she was done. With her paper napkin, she daubed her lips like a socialite then kissed me on the forehead.

"Excuse me a moment, I need to use a bathroom I can actually turn around in."

Mama D was impressed. She offered me a 10% discount and begged me to bring the girl back. I promised I would, God willing.

So went my days and nights. I was happier than I'd ever been. I couldn't share that happiness with my mother because she was north of the Arctic Circle stalking the polar bear, walrus, reindeer and bearded seal. I called Mr. Hamilton to see if we could get together, my treat, to thank him for all his help.

His wife answered. "John's in Washington but he'll be back in Pequot Falls in a week, late at night on November 8th. He is going hunting with some friends the next morning—the morning of the 9th. I'm sure he would be tickled pink if you joined them. They are going out early—6AM."

I told her, being new to the job I couldn't get time off for two months. "You know, Mrs. Hamilton, I wouldn't have this job and really I wouldn't even have this girlfriend if it wasn't for your husband."

"Tobias, John loves you like a son."

John Hamilton loved me like a son. That's how I got this job at the *Boston Globe*. He could do that because I'd been to Dartmouth College. John Hamilton got me into Dartmouth, and on the strength of a rousing, patriotic and wholly fictional recommendation, sent me off to the prestigious Gemma Institute. He had not chosen me to follow his files last week, or even the year before. The man had been guiding my life for a decade. Did he know ten years ago what he knows now, or did he know that some time he was going to need a chosen one? He had rules alright, ten of them. Mr. Hamilton drove those into me like he was giving me a new backbone, which, now that I can look back and see it all, he was. I stretched out on my polka-dot sofa, stared mindlessly out my window at the blank brick wall and slid back ten years to the warm days and nights in mother's summer cabin in Pequot Falls, NH.

3

I'M STILL STOUT, but not like I was as a child. Entering the sixth grade, the school nurse documented that I stood exactly five feet tall and weighed 182 pounds. A chubby biscuit of a boy. If I had had any brothers or sisters, I probably would have been more active; done things with them like ride bicycles around or play baseball or build a fort in a tree in the backyard—things that got me out of the house and away from the cookie jar—cookies I didn't have to share with anyone.

My mother spent most of her parenting hours trying to get me to have friends and do what they did. It didn't work. I preferred to sit in my room and read. She has always been an everyday jogger. She tried to convince me to jog along with her on walking trails that connected the parks in our town outside of Boston, Massachusetts. I found the notion frightening. Kids from my school lived along those paths and hung out in those parks. She swapped my cookies for granola bars, left plates of raw broccoli and little carrots on the kitchen counter and filled the refrigerator with yogurt and skim milk. None of it took. I bought more cookies at the bakery in town and kept them in my room. I liked oatmeal raisin the best. But when I was thirteen something happened that began the long process of coming to know myself, of finding truths and facing them.

I was three years old when my father died. He was an Army officer who died in a place called Bosnia-Herzegovina. Very few American's died there, but he was one of them. He'd been on a United Nations peacekeeping mission when his helicopter crashed in a mountain pass. Everybody was killed. That's what my mother told me. I didn't know him.

I only remember the men in uniform carrying a coffin to a graveyard, folding up a flag, lowering the casket into a hole, playing a trumpet, shoveling dirt on it and a man in a robe talking. One of the soldiers gave my mother the flag. It hangs on a pole on the screen porch of our summer home in Pequot Falls, New Hampshire.

Sitting on that porch, you can see the Presidential Range of the White Mountains. The mountains aren't all that high, but the winter weather is so severe Special Forces train there for high altitude warfare. In the fall the range is a blast of color as the leaves change to red, orange and gold. The summers are warm, and a velvet green extends up to the tree line above which nothing grows—greyish white granite rock to the peaks.

The presidents you can see are Washington, Jefferson, Adams, Lincoln and Garfield. There are other presidents out of sight and there are other mountains that are named for famous people, not presidents, like Mt. Clay and Mt. Lafayette, but I didn't care about them. Some days, I would sit for hours in a wicker chair beside my daddy's flag, looking off to those mountains wondering why it was that those people sent men off to die someplace so far from home. Each craggy peak became that man in my mind. My own uncarved Rushmore.

In the back of the house in a screened-in porch is a game room: Clue, Monopoly, Parcheesi, cards, a table that always had a half-done jig-saw puzzle on it, books, maps, and, in the corner, out of the way, a dart board. The summer I turned thirteen, trials for mass murder began in Bosnia. Mrs. Stone, the wife of the local police chief, who came each morning to jog with my mother, was talking about it; how ugly, unthinkable it all was. After they left, I took the dart board, covered it in a map of Europe, put Bosnia in the bull's eye, hung it on the front porch by my father's flag and threw darts at it. For hours I threw those darts until I got so good I could cluster them in a quarter-sized circle around a city called Sarajevo. That's where he died — somewhere near there.

This time, when my mother came home from her jog on Seven Sisters Trail, she didn't let me be. She walked up the porch steps, leaned against a post, stared at the dart board and began crying. Crying and wiping her eyes with her sleeve. I put my hand on her arm. She hugged me, brought me inside while she washed her face. She put her arm around my shoulder and walked me down the road to Mr. Hamilton's house. She told me to sit on his front steps and she went into the house alone. I knew Mr. Hamilton and his wife. Sometimes they came over and had drinks and played card games on the screened-in porch with my mother, Chief Stone and his wife and a State Police Trooper. I didn't know why Mr. Hamilton's friends were all policemen—it seemed strange. Mr. Hamilton wasn't all that old, but he was surely too old to be a policeman. His face was wrinkled, and he was stooped over when he walked. Not much, but not straight-up like a policeman.

My mother didn't come out of the house. Only Mr. Hamilton did. She must have left by the back door. I didn't see her until I got home. Mr. Hamilton brought me into his den and asked me to open the doors on a big cabinet. They wouldn't open. They were locked. He left the room and came back in with a key and opened both doors.

"Always keep them locked up," he said. He took a rifle out of the cabinet.

4

ON NOVEMBER 8, 2017 when I was at the dive bar near City Hall and got the phone call to go to the Sir John Motel, I had been following up leads on Jimmy Frocinone. One woman at the table in the bar seemed to know a lot about the way the leases were structured and how the projects naming rights and sponsorships were sold. And Trump was one of the major players in that market. Another girl, a wee bit of a thing with an impish face who worked in the mayor's office, kept talking in a hushed but squeaky tone about a porn star shacking up with Trump at one of Jimmy Frocinone's downtown hotels. I was getting somewhere. I thought my boss would be pleased—a few weeks in the office and I had a couple of leads. Then the phone got handed to me.

When I left the motel, there were a lot of things that were really disturbing. What was Mr. Hamilton talking about? Too dangerous to give to anybody? How could that be? But equally disturbing was the question of who the woman in the motel room was. It seemed clear she had been told by someone exactly how to let me see and hear the CD and told that it was to be destroyed after I had seen it. But she saw it too. Didn't that mean that she was a friend of Mr. Hamilton's? Or at least an associate? She had to be someone he trusted. She was in the video, sitting by the pool with a lot of other women in bikinis. And what's the story with that Navy Seal? Jesus, you don't have to have the world's most dangerous bouncer at a six-room flea-bag motel. None of it was making sense. I drove Rte. 1 from the motel back into downtown Boston. I kept slamming the brakes on. I was so distracted in my thoughts I couldn't seem to see the red lights until I was on them. Just concentrate, Tobias, just concentrate on your driving. Get home.

I couldn't park my mother's car in my neighborhood—it had no sticker and would surely get towed. I didn't want to be in Maggie's bar without her. Daddy James didn't seem to like me at all, but I had no choice. I needed his help.

"Hello, Mr. James. Do you remember me?"

"Where's my daughter?"

"I don't know, sir, I haven't seen her today. I'm here to ask you a favor."

"You're gonna ask me a favor? Is that what you said?"

"Yes, sir. It's important."

"Tell me about it."

I was not going to do that, so I just said, "I need to park my car here. If I don't, if it get's towed, if I can't get to work tomorrow, some innocent person may end up dying."

He smiled a crooked smile underneath a crooked nose and said, "That's balls." He reached in a drawer under the counter and handed me a Handicap placard. "Park out front. Put this on the mirror. You'll be fine." The misty rain on the walk home was soothing.

It was almost midnight and I still couldn't sleep. Every time I thought I had something cracked, I just came back around to the same questions that had no answers. The bars didn't close until two, so I decided to go down the street to a quiet place and have a beer. Quiet. *Don't think, just let it come to you. It will.*

McGowan's is a special bar. Tourists don't go there. The younger crowd doesn't go there. They go to loud places with younger music or live Irish music and sports events on wide screens. McGowan's doesn't have any of that. Just one small TV in the corner running news all day and night. Old Bald Freddie with his black bowtie and bartender's apron had been serving beer there for forty-one years. It was a local place and tonight most locals were sound asleep. A few were asleep in booths at the back of the bar, but most were tucked in their beds at home. I decided to write down everything I knew, had seen or had heard. I had a journalist's skinny spiral ringed steno pad, a pencil and a bottle of Budweiser.

1. That woman knew I was at that bar near City Hall
2. The Sir John Motel is a revolting place next to a strip club
3. The Navy Seal's tattoo might have been a fake or a fluke. Maybe I invented it in my mind.
4. The woman was no nonsense
5. She was putting on pole dancer's clothes when I left
6. That doesn't mean she was a pole dancer

That was as far as I got when ABC's *Nightline* came on after midnight. One of the stories was about the FBI looking into allegations of Russian meddling in the American election. Anonymous sources were reporting that a very senior FBI agent had first-hand contact with a man who might be the mastermind behind a possible Kremlin—Trump connection. The agent was not identified. He was going to testify behind closed doors in a week. There was a shot of a scowling senator walking through a doorway with James Comey, the Director of the FBI. Another quick shot (it looked like a hand-held smart phone video) of a man in some other place getting out of a black limousine. It looked like Mr. Hamilton. Was that possible? Then it quickly switched back to the anchor. It faded out with an aerial view of the FBI headquarters and ominous music. Sounded like Wagner. Spooky. I asked Bald Freddie for another Bud and added a few more notes.

7. The video was of a guy with links to Putin and Trump
8. The guy was in Kiev, England and Red Square
9. He was Israeli
10. His license plate number was AV16 PBR
11. Find the curly-headed man—expose him
11. Can't give anyone my files—too dangerous
12. Find my files   FIND MY FILES!!

I sat tapping my pencil on the counter, staring at my notes.

"Freddie, if my boss told me to go back and look into the Kennedy assassination and I found out that there was an FBI agent who actually interviewed Oswald before Ruby shot him and that agent had files that prove one hundred per cent that Oswald didn't shoot Kennedy, should I tell my boss what I found out or just publish the files?"

"You nuts, little boy? That's not news. Everybody knows Oswald didn't do it. FBI shot him. This beer's on me. Where's that girl of yours? She's a pistol."

When I got back to my apartment, I put my steno pad in the tiny freezer in my tiny refrigerator under a pound of bacon, locked the windows, locked the door, jammed one of my chairs under the knob, curled up very alone on my narrow bed, and went to sleep. Very alone.

It was four in the morning when I woke up drenched in sweat. Images of a dream were stuck in the corner of my mind—too far from reality to get a clean fix on it but close enough to see the bear, murky and big coming out of the woods toward Mr. Hamilton. It seemed foggy. He was smoking his pipe and leaning against the car, his back to the bear. It was a black limousine.

Four in the morning was too early to call Mr. Hamilton. His wife said he was getting in late last night, going out hunting with two friends at six this morning. Hunting is usually over by nine. At lunchtime, I'll pick up my mother's car and call Mr. Hamilton. I went back to sleep. When I woke again it was daylight—drizzly and overcast—and I was late for work.

Mornings in a newsroom are busy times. The paper is out, and people have read it. They call in with tips, with outrage, with thanks and with demands for corrections. My father's name was Eduard, not Edward. The DA did not say, "We are pursuing a homicide conviction," he said, "We are looking at pursuing a homicide conviction." The news people haven't yet gone out on their assignments and everyone is moving fast, fired up with coffee and anticipation.

Jasmine, our stupendous young secretary, was on the phone with some poor sot who had been evicted from his rent-controlled apartment on a trumped-up drug allegation. I could hear her—her voice was soothing, coaxing—she even smiled and nodded as he went on and on about his sad circumstance. She looked over at the corner office, pointed to my cubicle and flicked her hand as if to say, "Go sit down before he comes around." Just in time. Sam Borstien was starting to make his rounds, issuing an order here, a little advice there, a pat on the back or a growl.

"You got anything, Tobias?"

"Yes, sir. Trump Organization is working with Frocinone on the branding of two hotels. Nothing funny about it yet, but the Trump people got in touch with them, not the other way around. There's something out there that has to do with Trump and porn stars. I haven't got a fix on it yet. Frocinone's people don't seem to want to have anything to do with it. Scared off by all the news, probably, but I'll keep digging."

"Okay, dig deep on this one. Remember the Emoluments Clause but really dig down on the porn star stuff. That's good."

"Yes, sir, but there is something else."

"Yeah, what?"

I looked around. All three other cubicle mates had stopped working. They were listening. "Could we talk in your office. Is that possible?"

Here's where it all came down. Everything I'd learned and heard about confidentiality of sources. Shielded from whom? Everybody in the world? Only law enforcement? Your boss? Can you trust your boss not to let it go out to anyone? His boss? No, I thought as I found my way into the chair in front of his desk, fidgeting with my pencil. In the corner, cable news murmured quietly from a small television. No, I can't let it out. I remembered Mr. Hamilton's voice, *Don't let* anyone *know what you have seen and heard here.* He said, *anyone.*

"Mr. Borstien, I need a few days off the Frocinone connection. I need to work on something else. It is related to Trump. It's from a personal source I have, but I really can't talk to anyone about it for a few days at least. Can I have until Monday?"

"No, not if you're unwilling to tell me what it is you're pursuing. I don't need to know your source's name, but I do need to know the context. Otherwise, no."

I sat flicking my pencil on the arm of the chair, trying to figure out how to get him to say 'yes' without getting fired in the process. Maybe, that's what it was going to be. Best to get fired standing tall. Tell him the truth without revealing anything of confidence.

"Mr. Borstien, I believe I have to do this even if I lose my job. It is very important to me. It is an obligation I have to a good friend and it is also newsworthy and important politically. Can you reconsider?"

We both sat for a moment. His look had changed. He leaned forward and put his chin in his palm, contemplating me. I heard a name on the TV and stood up staring at the screen.

"Early this morning, a senior FBI agent, John Cabot Hamilton, was killed in a hunting accident in Pequot Falls, New Hampshire. The New Hampshire Department of Fish and Game is leading the investigation. A statement from Major Littlefield, the law enforcement director of the department, issued from Concord, New Hampshire this morning at 8:30 AM confirms that Mr. Hamilton was accidentally shot by a young hunter who mistook him for a deer. He stated that no charges have been filed. Our affiliate, WMUR of Manchester, New Hampshire is sending reporters to Pequot Falls. We will keep you advised as more is known about the circumstances."

I was trembling. "I have to go now. That was my friend. That was my friend. That is the man I have to talk to today. I have to talk to him but now he's dead. My friend is dead, Mr. Borstien." I left his office, stumbled past my cubicle, past Jasmine and out into the November drizzle.

5

I TURNED MY COAT COLLAR UP, jammed my hands in my pockets and walked into the damp breeze, not seeing any of the other people on the street. My eyes were turned down toward the sidewalk. I saw legs and shoes and puddles and occasionally I would bump someone, mutter "Excuse me," shift a bit and keep walking. Maggie was not in the Registrar of Deeds. She was in a training seminar across town. I wrote a note—*Got to go to Pequot Falls. A friend died. Back in a few days*—and left it with her assistant.

I walked along the edge of Boston Common, past the Wilbur, past the Royale and down to Winchester Street. The car was still there. No ticket on the windshield. The handicap placard was still on the mirror. There was a brand-new parking permit for my neighborhood in Southie. It was on the inside of the window. The cops had opened the door, put it there and re-locked the door. Holy Mackerel, Daddy sure had a lot of pull in this town. The bar signs were still unlit, but the front door was open. I poked my head in. A janitor was mopping the floor, stools upended on the bar counter.

"Mr. James here?" I asked.

"Nope. Half hour."

"Can you give him a message?"

"Sure."

"Tobias Starkey says thank you."

"You got it," and he went back to swinging his mop.

I-93 N is an easy drive. Up through Massachusetts into New Hampshire, past Manchester and Concord and into the foothills of the White Mountains with sweeping panoramas of the north country ahead. That's why it's such a soothing drive. Make your way past the hubbub of the cities and all that lies ahead are simple villages nestled into peaceful places. All the tension eases off. I didn't really know why I was going there today—there would be no memorial service set up yet, the hunting accident would still be under investigation and nobody would be saying anything. What good could I do? Perhaps just tell Mrs. Hamilton how sorry I am and offer to help in any way she wants. At the least, I had to do that, but maybe just that, and then come home.

The key was where it always was; under the flagpole stand. I stood on the porch staring at the flag, remembering that it was that flag that had triggered all the pain and loneliness of living without a father, triggered the anger, the map and dart board and it was that flag that brought me to Mr. Hamilton. John Cabot Hamilton, my hunting teacher, my mentor, a very senior FBI agent. I never asked him what he did for work. It's probably just as well I didn't know. It might have changed our relationship and that would have been bad. It was perfect how it was.

I had never been in my summer home alone. My mother had always been here with me. She must have always turned on the electricity, heat and water, aired the house out and made the beds—all without me even knowing she did these things. It was stuffy inside, but a good stuffy. It smelled like a closed-up cabin. I opened a few windows. I found the electric panel and flipped the main breaker on. Blankets and sheets were in a cedar trunk in my mother's bedroom. I wandered around the house, looking at things that had always been there and I had never taken the time to see. Over the fireplace was a photo of my mother and father on their wedding day—gowns and flowers and happy, laughing people. A photo of my father in his army uniform with lots of badges and stripes hung on the wall nearby. I wondered if my mother would remove these and put them in a box somewhere if her boyfriend Gilbert ever came up here. No, she wouldn't. She would leave them right where they were, and he could either get over it or leave. She was tough like that. I went to sleep. My dreams were full of city noise, loud noise and someone, probably Mr. Borstien, was a large dog—all jowls and drool.

In the morning, I puttered. I puttered the morning away, poking around at the jigsaw puzzle, sorting out the silverware into perfect sets. I knew I was puttering, trying to avoid going to see Mrs. Hamilton. I didn't want to go see her. I didn't know her all *that* well, but I realized that if I owed anybody anything in this world, I owed her the courtesy of my condolences. Mr. Hamilton would have told me that that was at the core of growing up.

Her car was in the driveway. She came to the door and hugged me close. Her face was stained with tears and her cheeks were red from rubbing and wiping them away. She was alone in her house. Maybe neighbors or friends had been there, but they were gone now. She brought me an iced tea and had me sit in the living room while she went in search of something. She came back with a cardboard box sealed tight with packing tape.

"Before John went to Washington last week, he said that if you happened to come visit, then this was for you. A gift. He was truly fond of you." She handed it to me and pointed out the window at a stump in the yard. There had been a toaster all shot full of holes sitting on top of that stump.

"Thank you. I told him I wanted to make a piece of art out of it. I guess he didn't forget that, but why would he have thought I might come here when he wasn't here?"

"Tobias, I don't know the answer to that, but over the last few weeks he had been doing unusual things—working late nights on his computer, burning things in the fireplace. I could smell it from the bedroom. Cleaning up as though he knew something might happen to him. I really don't know. He didn't say anything, but it all seemed a bit strange."

There was a loud three-beat knock at the front door. "Oh dear," she said, "I don't like the sound of that. That isn't very polite." She opened the door and two men were standing there, erect and grim faced.

"Mrs. Hamilton?"

"Yes?"

"I'm Special Agent Donovan and this is Agent Worthy. We're from the Concord office of the FBI and we've come to offer our condolences to you on behalf of the whole Bureau, including the director. We're deeply saddened. John was a good agent and a good man."

"Thank you, Special Agent Donovan. Thank you both very much. That was kind of you to stop by. I have a visitor here I must return to but thank you again for coming here with your kind thoughts and thank also Director Comey."

"Mrs. Hamilton, could we come in for just a minute? There is something we need to discuss." The man was nudging past her, moving into the house.

"Would you both please leave now? I lost my husband yesterday and I would like to grieve however I wish. Now please go away." She was beginning to sob.

Both agents crossed the hall and stood in front of me. The Donovan guy put his hand on his hip, moving his jacket open so that I would see the gun in his shoulder holster. He had very bushy eyebrows and a large nose. The other guy was tall and skinny, but kind of mousey looking.

"Who are you?"

"My name is Tobias Starkey and I am a friend from down the road," I stammered.

"What is in the box?"

This was getting scary. They weren't here to be nice to Mrs. Hamilton. "I don't know for sure. I haven't opened it yet but it's a gift for me from Mr. Hamilton. I think it's a busted toaster."

He snapped his fingers and Agent Worthy fished in his pocket and handed him a pocket knife. He flipped the blade open, took the box out of my hands, slit the packing tape and pulled out my toaster.

"What the hell is this?"

"It's my toaster."

He pulled a note out of one of the bread slice holes. "What does this mean, 'Thoroughly clean before curating'?" He handed me the note.

"Agent Donovan, curating means showing as an art piece. Now, if you're going to arrest me or confiscate my toaster, then do it. If not, give it back to me and leave. Mrs. Hamilton doesn't want you here."

"Thank you, Tobias."

He stared at it, turned it over, shook it and peered into the slice holes He gave me back my toaster. "Mrs. Hamilton, where are John's files?"

"I have no idea. He said he put them in his sister's barn and the barn burned down. They aren't here, of that I'm certain."

He snapped his fingers again at Agent Worthy and put his thumb and finger to his ear and mouth. "Call it in. Find the sister. Did she have a barn that burned? Mrs. Hamilton, may we have a look around the house, please. It won't take long."

"Do you two have a warrant?" She had stopped sobbing and turned hard.

Special Agent Donovan reached into his jacket pocket, pulled out his wallet badge, flipped it open and said, "This is all the warrant I need. Those files are the property of the Federal Bureau of Investigation and we are here to collect them. Now, we need to have a look around just to make sure that what you say is true. So, if you don't mind…". He pointed to the front door.

Mrs. Hamilton pulled herself up to her full 5'-2" height and glared up at the man. "You two seem to think you can do anything you want. That's not very attractive for a public servant. Aside from that, it's illegal. I'm going to a neighbor's house. I'll be back in half an hour. If you're not gone by then, I will have the police arrest you for trespassing, and don't for a minute think they can't or won't. They can, and they will. Tobias, please come with me. Thirty minutes, not a minute longer." She spun and walked out the door.

On the front step, she asked me, in a loud voice, to drive her to Chief Stone's house. In the driveway she turned and yelled, "And stay out of my underwear drawer, you miserable perverts!"

They wanted the files. The files that Mr. Hamilton told me to find. I thought for a moment I should tell Mrs. Hamilton about the

CD I watched in the Sir John Motel, then realized that is exactly what Mr. Hamilton didn't want to have happen. He somehow knew that sooner or later these two guys, or guys just like them, would come for the files and it was important that neither Jane Hamilton nor I, nor anyone else, knew where those files were. He didn't want the FBI to find them. These guys might just beat it out of somebody if they thought that somebody knew where the files were. I guessed that when he made that CD, he hadn't made up his mind about where to put them or, maybe, he didn't want the pole dancer to know where he had hidden them. Wherever the files were, there would be a clue somewhere that pointed me in the right direction without ever recording or writing down where that place was. I was scared. Mrs. Hamilton was mad. What a hell of a way to be on the day after your husband dies.

"Tobias, please just drive me around for a half-hour. I don't want to go to Chief Stone's house. There is nothing he can do and I'm not so sure I trust him about all of this. Drive that way, please." She pointed east. I drove down to an intersection, turned right and drove into the next town over. I turned right at some lights and onto a wooden bridge that spanned a river.

"That's where Robert Frost taught English when he was young," she said as we passed by large, square building. "John loved his poetry. He read it aloud to me all the time. So simple, so graceful," and she pulled a handkerchief from her purse and wiped the tears away.

"Mrs. Hamilton, do you mind if I ask who your husband was going hunting with."

"It was Chief Stone and a friend of John's from South Boston. A fellow FBI agent named Jim Lacey. He has a summer house here out by Casket Pond. A nice enough man but they say he's a hard drinker.

They apparently never showed up to hunt. Both of them came to the house yesterday. Chief Stone said he slept late, and Agent Lacey said he was hunting alone on the other side of the mountain. They were the ones who came to tell me John was dead. I must admit I got a bit hysterical, screaming and wailing, but all in all, it seems to me their sorrow was hollow. Forced, somehow. They kept looking at their feet and the walls. John would have looked me right in the eye."

I drove through the woods and hills and back to her house in Pequot Falls. There was no one there. The house was closed. I walked her to the door. She hugged me again and said, "Thank you, Tobias, I'll be fine. Do you have your toaster?"

"Yes, Mrs. Hamilton, it's in my car. Are you sure you're going to be okay?"

"Oh, yes, I'll be okay. My sister is coming tonight to stay with me. Tobias," she held me by the shoulders, "my husband knew something that he didn't want anyone else to know. I don't know what that is, he never spoke of it. Those men were not John's people. They wanted me to think they were. Director Comey would have called ahead if he knew they were coming here. Those two men were FBI alright, but they were rogue agents sent by somebody else. My home will be as though they were never here. Clean and spotless. No fingerprints. Any door that was locked, they will have just picked it and re-locked it. If I call Washington, the FBI will back up their story because they've been told to do so. And oh, oh, oh would the FBI apologize for them being so mean to a grieving widow." She touched me on the cheek. "They're not my husband's people, they were sent by some other agency, probably the CIA."

"My God, Mrs. Hamilton, this is so sad. I'm so sorry."

"That poor young man, Tom Duncan. That's who we should feel sorry for."

"Tom Duncan? He's my age. I met him. Was he...?'

"Yes. It makes me sick at heart. They say he mistook John for a deer. The poor boy thinks he shot my husband."

I unmade the bed, put the sheets, blankets and pillows back in the cedar trunk, closed the windows, shut off the water, shut off the heater and all the electricity, locked the door and put the key back under my father's flag. I was out of that town. Back down the long highway through the foothills of the Presidential Range. There was no way I was staying there with those guys lurking around. I was gone like a cool breeze. Seventy-five miles an hour down the highway back to Boston. Back to my tiny apartment. Back to Maggie? Back to work? What?

Something disturbed my soul. How was it even possible John Hamilton died in a hunting accident? When it came to guns and hunting, he was the most careful, the most conscientious and thorough hunter imaginable. He had taught me that, if I followed his rules, I could also be a first-class woodsman, rifleman and hunter, just like him. And he was a lawman, an FBI agent. They are not known for making mistakes when they have a gun in their hand. It made no sense that he would die hunting in the woods he knew so well. My God, I think he knew every tree and twig. How could it be? My eyes were on the road, but my mind was in the past, remembering all his rules. Ten of them—stern, certain and clear.

6

THAT SUMMER WHEN I WAS THIRTEEN, when my mom had led me down the road to Mr. Hamilton's house and then disappeared out the back door, he had taken a rifle out of his gun cabinet and led me out to his front porch.

Rule #1: *Always Keep Your Guns Locked Up* and keep the key either in your pocket or hidden where a child, a criminal or an angry spouse can't find it. Keep the ammunition locked separately. There were six guns in the cabinet, all standing upright, side by side, all shiny.

Rule #2: *Know Your Gun.* My training began there with a Remington Woodsmaster 742, sitting on his porch, listening as he explained what all the parts were called and how they worked. Taking it apart. Oiling it. Putting it back together. Taking it apart.

Rule #3: *Always Keep the Muzzle Pointed in a Safe Direction*, not at Mrs. Hamilton when she comes out on the porch with glasses of iced tea. When we were done with that first lesson, he asked me to put the gun back. He told me it was his favorite gun, but it was my gun from now on. A gift from him to me, but until I was old enough, it would stay locked in his gun cabinet. I could use it any time I came up to Pequot Falls provided I learned how to handle it. He said he was going to teach me how to do that and then he was going to teach me how to hunt.

"Hunt? Hunt what?"

"Deer."

"I don't want to shoot a deer, Mr. Hamilton."

"Hunting is not necessarily shooting. You don't have to shoot if you don't want to, or," he looked at me sternly, "you don't have to pull the trigger unless you have to pull the trigger. Important distinction."

Rule #4: *Dress and Pack Properly for the Weather and Topography – Plan Ahead.* Conformance with this rule required an early departure for a three-hour drive with my mother through the middle of the White Mountain National Forest, climbing up to 3,500 feet then down across the state of Maine to the Atlantic Ocean to L.L. Bean's in the town of Freeport which, according to her, was the only store in America that sold appropriate woods clothing.

The Bean Boots, which are rubber, were on display past the canoes and carved and painted mallard decoys under a sign that said, "The World's Best Duck Hunting Boots," but I didn't argue. I didn't point out that I wasn't going duck hunting. I just wanted to go home. We bought a pair. I asked the clerk if they stretched, being rubber, because my feet were growing a size a year. No, they don't. We also bought a genuine L.L. Bean quilted red and black checkered hunting jacket, just like Mr. Hamilton's, a matching red and black checkered wool hunting cap with ear flaps that made me look like a miniature Ignatius J. Reilly from *A Confederacy of Dunces*, a pair of super stiff waterproof canvas pants with a dozen pockets, a six inch bone-handled knife for slicing open a deer's belly or cutting marks in tree bark so you don't get lost, a leather sheathe with an antlered deer embossed on it, two pairs of wool socks and a mesh food bag with a long shoulder strap.

"There you go," she said when we got outside, tussling my hair, "ready to go hunting." I straightened out my hair, looking around the parking lot for kids my age. "Can we go home now?" The sun had set when we got back to Pequot Falls.

Rule #5: *Be Quiet, Careful and Always Aware of Your Surroundings.* Mr. Hamilton dropped me off at the end of Old Stonehouse Road. He spread out his topographic map on the hood of his Jeep.

"We're here", he said pointing to a place on the map. "You're going here," he said tapping a place that said, 'Black Bear Hill - El. 1615'. "Do you see that hill over there to the south? That's it. We're at elevation 1310' so you have about a three-hundred-foot climb. That's where you're going. What time does your watch have?"

We calibrated our watches to the minute.

"Remember how I told you to set your compass? Let's see you do it."

I fished it out of one of my many pockets, steadied the north arrow and lined up my destination by setting the black stripe on the top of the hill.

"Good." He folded up the map and gave it to me. "It's about a mile. I'll meet you back here in exactly two hours. Check your safety."

I pushed the safety button behind the trigger, first in, then out again, pointed the gun barrel at the ground ten feet in front of me and gently squeezed the trigger. It didn't move. It was locked. The safety was on.

Rule #6: *Never Put Your Finger on The Trigger (or even inside the trigger guard) Until You Are Ready to Shoot.* Do not walk with a loaded gun. Do not load a round in the magazine until you are settled in and stationary. Do not trust the safety but always check it. Do not release it to 'off' until your quarry is in sight. Do not squeeze the trigger until you are 100% certain of what your target is—you can see it clearly enough to know that it is what you think it is—and you have a clean shot. Do not guess with a loaded rifle.

He drove off. I was, for the first time in my life, completely alone in a strange and foreboding place. I stood still, listening for the sounds of creatures skulking around. I didn't want to go into those woods all by myself. Who knows what can happen? My mother's house was only about five miles away. I could walk there in a couple of hours…then what would I say to my mother? What would I say to Mr. Hamilton? What would I say to myself?

I adjusted my food bag, pulled my new cap down firmly on my head, checked the handle snap on my knife sheathe, got my rifle pointed down and slightly off to the side and set off concentrating hard on where the soles of my new Bean Boots were supposed to be. I had practiced this walking in the woods behind Mr. Hamilton's house in the morning when it was damp with dew and in the late afternoon when it was hot and dry and twigs snapped. I'd practiced in the night with no light. He taught me to find my way along a trail in the dark, a trail I couldn't see, by listening to the sound of my boots on the path. If there were only pine needles and leaves on the trail—the walk was quiet. When I would step off the trail, it made a crunching sound and I would back up a step and try it again in a slightly different direction. I was amazed that I could follow that path with just my ears. Mr. Hamilton showed me how to build a shallow hut with bent boughs, so if I did get lost, I could sleep in the woods until daylight. Cut the boughs off with a steep slice so you can stick them in the ground and weave the tops together.

Step only where the forest floor is soft with leaves or pine needles. Don't step on twigs. In the early autumn morning just before the sun rises, the forest is like a painting: immobile, mute. It is the space between the owls of the night and the hawks of the day when soft rays of pinkish light begin to slice between the tree trunks. Don't bend back a dry branch. The snap will break like a rifle shot. The deer will bolt. Eastern White tail deer can go from stock-still to a full bounding sprint in the blink of an eye. Their tails flick up—the 'white flag'—then they're gone. They're 'high-tailing it.' That's why you must be careful about the path you choose. Make sure your clothes are tucked in and buttoned so they don't snag on branches and make sure nothing white is showing.

Rule #7: *Don't Wear Any Visible White*. You might not be alone out there. Don't look like a deer. Don't look like a white flag.

When I came to a tree or rock, I would stop, look around, pick a path that had the fewest twigs in it and swing the barrel whichever way I thought it least likely that anything would be hiding or walking about. I kept my finger along the side of the gunstock making sure it didn't slip into the trigger guard. I don't know why it was so important that morning. The gun wasn't loaded, and I didn't have any bullets on me. It was August, two months before hunting season. I was in training. I still hadn't touched or even seen a bullet. I did everything I thought Mr. Hamilton would want me to do. I checked my compass every little once in a while, corrected course, and trudged on. The water bottle my mother had packed for me in my new mesh bag had leaked all over my tuna fish sandwiches and down the front of my brand new canvas pants. By the time I got to where I was supposed to be, at the rock outcropping on top of Black Bear Hill, the wet pants had chaffed the inside of both thighs, my new left boot had worn a raw spot on my ankle, my head itched underneath my floppy-eared wool hat, my arm ached from carrying my rifle just so. But I made it. Five minutes early. I made it. Me, alone, a mile in the woods. I did it.

I sat back against a rock and smiled to myself. I did it! The sun had risen, daylight spread through the forest. The stillness in the air settled over me, around me like a blanket. One small plume of white smoke rose from a cabin chimney a few miles off. Down the hill in front of me, running crosswise, the grasses were beaten down in a narrow stip. That must be where the deer walk. It can't be people way out here. That is what Mr. Hamilton was talking about—'tell me if it's a good place to hunt.' Well, yes, Mr. Hamilton, it is a very good place to hunt. I watched a squirrel scamper up an oak and fidget about in the acorns then scamper half-way down and stop stock still, not blinking, not even a twitch of the nose as a hawk glided low over the edge of the hill not far from the tree. I thought I heard a quiet breath from the feathered wings passing through warming air. In that instant the squirrel was not a squirrel, it was a knot-lump, a brown carbuncle on tree bark. The big bird canted slightly and swept off down the valley and off to another mountain ridge. The squirrel chattered and dashed for the ground.

I sat up with a jolt. I checked my watch. I was five minutes late. I had to go now, back to the road. Where was the road? Which way down? Where did I come from? I stood, slowly turning in a circle trying to remember which tree I might have walked past. They were all the same. I forgot to cut notches. Had the white smoke been ahead of me or behind me when I was coming up here? Mr.

Hamilton! Mr. Hamilton! I screamed out. Nothing, just the chatter of squirrels.

Rule #8: *Always Know Where You Are* and how to get back to where you came from. On the way in, identify landmarks or cut notches in tree bark so you can find your way out. One of the most dangerous things is to get lost in the woods. Not just because you might never get out or never get found and die of dehydration or starvation or get attacked by a bear, but because when you first realize you're lost, you tend to panic and when you panic you forget all the rules you've been taught, then you are really in trouble.

Rule #9: *Never Panic*, not even when you accidently shoot another human being. Not even when you fall and break your leg, not even when there is a huge black bear sniffing the air and coming right at you. Even when you're lost, do not panic, use your compass, that's what he taught me to do.

I unfolded the map and laid it flat on the ground, I put my compass on the map, turning the map until the north arrow lined up with the arrow on my compass, Here I am on Black Bear Hill and here is the end of Old Stonehouse Road, that way.

Are you allowed to step on twigs on your way out of the forest? Yes, you've already shot a deer or you're not going to. You don't care if you scare them all away, and you're fifteen minutes late. I headed downhill at nearly a trot, breaking branches and paying no attention to what my new Bean Boots were stepping on.

I found the road, but I didn't know which way it was to the end where Mr. Hamilton parked his Jeep. I pulled out the map and aligned the road with the road on the map. The end was to my left.

Mr. Hamilton was leaning against the hood, smoking his pipe, reading a book. He patted me on the shoulder.

"Very good job, Tobias. You get an 'A.'"

Rule #10: *Fishermen Lie, Hunters Don't.* If you saw it clearly enough to count the antler prongs and say it was a huge ten-point buck that got away, then either you're a lousy shot and shouldn't be out there hunting or you violated at least one of the above Rules and shouldn't be out there hunting. If you made it up, you're not a good hunter; if you didn't make it up, you're not a good hunter. Don't get caught in that trap. Don't lie. About anything.

I told Mr. Hamilton about how I panicked.

"Good hunters bring food that bears can't smell or don't eat, like granola bars in their wrapper or carrots or maybe broccoli in a zip-lock bag — never tuna fish or peanut butter. They can smell that a mile away."

"You've been talking to my mom."

"Yep, I have. Very smart of you to throw away your bag of food before you headed down the hill."

"You were watching me?"

"Of course. It was your first time out. Next time, solo."

We drove away in his Jeep, both of us silent for a while. "On second thought, Tobias, you get an 'A+'. That's because you realized you were in danger, which you were, brought your panic under control, remembered what you were supposed to do, and did it very quickly. I'm proud of you."

"I was in danger? Really?"

"Yes, a bear did come and eat your lunch not more than a few minutes after you left. She was waiting for you to leave. I saw her."

Sunday morning, I was up early and off to Mr. Hamilton's house. He invited me for breakfast and a lesson on ammunition. He had to leave Pequot Falls by noon and didn't want our training momentum to stall. Sitting in his den, I could hear him in the kitchen. I smelled smoke.

"Goddamit!"

What do you do to fix a vintage, stainless steel two-slice Toastmaster that has burned your English muffins to a blackened crisp three days in a row? What do you do when the doohickey that adjusts how dark the muffin should be is broken and can't be repaired? You unplug it, grab it by the bread holes, carry it out across the field behind your house, put it on a tree stump, back up 100 feet, take your rifle and blow a hole right through it. Mr. Hamilton decided that this was the right thing to do and the perfect time to teach a young boy how to shoot a gun. Then, and this was the part that Mrs. Hamilton didn't like, you leave it there, so you can hurl insults at every time you see it.

Empty cartridge ejected, new one in the chamber, safety 'off', feet set solid, rifle stock pulled snug into my shoulder, leaning slightly forward trying to line up the toaster with the bead on the end of the barrel, trying to stop the barrel from wiggling around, I pulled the trigger too early and a hunk at the base of the stump flew off but.....it didn't knock me back on the ground. I stood standing. Three shots later I got it and we backed up another 200 feet. Aiming in the same place, I hit the top of the stump and got a long lecture on how altitude, temperature, wind, barometric pressure and distance affect the trajectory of a bullet.

"There's a breeze from the south, the barometer is probably just about 30, and the distance is now around 300 feet. Aim to the upper right quadrant."

I hit it dead center.

7

JOHN HAMILTON WAS A CATHOLIC. The funeral, in his hometown of Hudson, Massachusetts was short but dense. He was laid to rest in Saint Michael's Parish cemetery. I did not attend the burial. It was the first funeral I ever attended, and I drove away with the strong notion that I would avoid them in the future. I spent the next month trying my best to concentrate on work. Nothing came easy because nothing was fun. I shook out a lot of leads on the Trump - Frocinone connections but nothing solid enough to go to print. There was nothing I could do about following the leads Mr. Hamilton gave me and the quest for his files—which very well might have been found by the FBI in his sister's barn—until the case was closed. That should be the day Tom Duncan was found guilty or not guilty. The hearing was scheduled for December 7th, a month to the day after the shooting. Three days from now. I was getting itchy to find out what happened and whether it was just an unfortunate accident. Most of me hoped it was.

The toaster still sat in its box in my apartment. The next day I called in sick and spent all morning walking the streets. I found a log about two feet tall and eight inches in diameter on the side of the road where the power company had been cutting trees back away from the power lines. It was from a dead limb and the bark had peeled off. I put it on my shoulder and lugged it back to my apartment. I got a tube of chrome polish, a piece of sandpaper, a paint brush and a pint of shellac from the hardware store. I spread newspapers on the floor and sanded and painted the base to my very first piece of art. It was, more than anything, my own direct connection with my hunting instructor—now dead from a hunting accident. The painful irony of it all was so evident with every brush stroke. I was sitting cross-legged on the floor shining up the toaster with the polish, just as Mr. Hamilton said I should, when Maggie came in.

"No job today, Tobias? I called, and they said you hadn't come in."

"No, no job today. I'm taking some time off."

"And you don't think they'll maybe decide they don't need you?"

"They might, but I doubt it."

"And why is that?"

I told her who John Hamilton was and how he died. And I told her that there was something funny about that I needed to pay attention to. Things didn't add up.

"I'm really sorry to hear about your friend. You didn't tell me he was an FBI agent."

"I didn't know that about him until I heard it on the news."

She crossed her arms and stood looking down at me. "I am sorry for you, but is this how you find out what doesn't add up? By sitting on the floor polishing a worthless toaster that somebody shot the shit out of. That's getting you closer to figuring it all out?"

"Yes." I told her how the toaster got shot and about Mrs. Hamilton and the FBI and how they inspected it and gave it back. That they were there for Mr. Hamilton's files and that's what doesn't add up. I said I was sitting here thinking my way through it all, Zen-like. The note—*thoroughly clean before curating*—was on the table.

"Did you thoroughly clean it?"

"That, in case you missed it, is what I'm doing right now." My hackles were getting up but there was a fire in her eyes that dared me to take her on. I didn't.

"No, Tobias, I mean the inside. You have to clean the inside of things before you clean the outside or all the crud will get right back on it. Like the slice holes and the crumb tray. Those things first. She went to the kitchen and got a wet rag and a scrub brush, then sat beside me on the floor. I handed her the toaster and she up-ended it. Someone had already cleaned it and scrubbed the ten years of rust off it. She flipped open the crumb tray and there was a brown envelope taped to the inside of the tray. We both breathed deeply. "Uh-oh," she said. She peeled it off, handed it to me and leaned in close, putting her arm around my shoulder.

"Maggie, I think I need to read this by myself." She unfolded herself and walked into the bathroom.

Tobias,

I am truly sorry to have burdened you with this, but you are the only person I trust to do what must be done. You are young enough, so no one will suspect you. I am to testify behind closed doors to a Senate Select Committee on November 12th. I can't send the file—it might get intercepted. I can't bring it myself. There are powerful people who don't want me to testify, so I might not make it there. The steps I have taken, which I hope you can follow, are designed to protect the information the Senate wants, and our democracy desperately needs. I cannot tell you where you will find what

*you are looking for because someone else may read this first.
Follow my path to the end. Find the keeper of secrets. Also, if
you hear of my accidental death, do not believe it. It will have
been murder.*

Your friend for eternity,

John Cabot Hamilton   *Vox Clamantis in Deserto*
*Associate Director of the FBI for Counterintelligence and National
Security*

I sat, stunned. John Hamilton was murdered, and he knew it was
going to happen. He just didn't know who, where, when or how but
he did know why. Is that what Jane Hamilton meant about Tom
Duncan—'the poor boy thinks he shot my husband'?

"Hey, Maggie, can you come here?" She came and sat back down.
"You can read this if you want to. There is nothing secret in it. But
before you say yes, think about whether you want to stick with me
because it's going to get hard and could be dangerous. And I can't
tell you everything. It may be easier and better for you to walk away
right now. This is going to take a while. You were right about the
'uh-oh' part."

Maggie didn't hesitate. She took the note and read it. She walked
back into the bathroom and closed the door. A few minutes later she
came back and said, "Just because he thought it was possible he was
going to be murdered, doesn't mean he was. It really might have
been a hunting accident that happened at a coincidental time. Why
don't you put that stupid toaster on its stupid stump and let's get out
of here and go find out." Ponderous contemplation was not one of

Maggie's salient features, but a quick and open mind was. She was not a conspiracy theorist—they were mostly fools—she dealt in facts. I hugged her, held her for a long time until she wriggled free. "What is, *Vox Clamantis in Deserto?*"

"It's the Dartmouth motto. It means, *A voice crying out in the wilderness.* Don't ask me where that came from—nobody knows. Maybe the Bible. Maybe Indians begging to be converted to Christianity. But, you know, that's the first time I've seen it used where it actually might mean something."

Sam Borstien didn't bat an eye. Going up north was fine with him. The *New York Times* had sent a reporter to Pequot Falls. "Scoop 'em, young man, you got the inside dope." It struck me as a fake statement, as if he were imitating an old time, hard-drinking newspaper man. When I stopped by to tell Jasmine I was going away for a while she let on that the chief Washington correspondent was taking over the porn star story. Somebody had hit pay dirt on it. She asked if I had made certain with Borstien that I had a job when I got back—story or no story. I shook my head and she flicked her fingers toward his office. "Do it."

Sam Borstien turned his back to me, put his hands in his pockets and stood taking in the magnificent view of downtown Boston out of his corner office window. After a while of this urban contemplation, he said, "Scoop it," like he was talking to some lady on the street whose poodle was taking a crap on the sidewalk. When I passed Jasmine I just shook my head. She grimaced, then blew me a kiss. Some people are nice, some people aren't.

Maggie told her boss that there had been a death in the family and she needed to take her saved-up vacation time starting today.

She didn't say whose family was so suddenly bereaved, but she had gotten a consoling hug and an administrative approval.

"I read the Employee Manual before I talked to Ms. Alfaro," Maggie told me. "One of the reasons listed for granting immediate leave was 'family death.' It didn't say whose family." She was like that. All about the facts.

The Old South Ender was nearly full at four in the afternoon. The seven to three shift was out. Johnny James once again booted two fellows over to the side tables so his daughter could sit at the bar. She explained what had happened and told him she would be in New Hampshire for a while, maybe even a couple of weeks. Then she said something that hadn't occurred to me.

"If the police give us the documents—the accident and investigation reports, it is very likely it is just a hunting accident. But, if they refuse or stall or balk, it just might be something else."

"FBI agent went down, huh? I don't like it when cops go down."

"If we can't get the documents, maybe you could have the DA's office nudge them a little bit. Dan would do that for you, wouldn't he?"

"Maybe."

"Or Commissioner Peters. Both of them probably knew him, or of him anyway."

I said, "John Hamilton was a nationally important law enforcement officer and he was born and raised in Hudson, Massachusetts. A local guy. That might help."

"Might."

"Daddy, wasn't there a man who worked with Dan in the DA's office who used to come here a lot and then he went to the New Hampshire Attorney General's office? Tall, skinny man with black hair and glasses. He used to help me with my homework. He was really nice. You remember him?"

"Yeah. Al Somebody. Italian, from the North End."

"So, I can call you if we need a little help?"

"Maggie," he said leaning over the counter, "you can always call me." She kissed him on his crooked nose.

I looked down the length of the bar. In the first six or eight stools and most of the tables on the wall were neighborhood folks, mostly scraggy men, sallow and quiet, in there for the long haul. The next set of stools were mostly chunky guys. Lots of beer. The cops. Some others were still in great shape. I thought those were the firemen who had to climb up long ladders, haul heavy hoses and run up burning staircases without pooping out. There was a back area with just tables. Five or six men in suit jackets and loosened ties were there drinking mixed drinks. Probably the District Attorneys. Everyone was laughing and joking. The day was behind them and they came together in the late afternoon to do just this—drink, shoot the shit, and dull the senses enough so the night was tolerable. They all probably lived in neighborhoods with single family homes in need of paint and new porch railings. Homes with driveways where, after five or six beers, or whiskey and sodas at Johnny James' place, they would pull up, park, see the BBQ grill lid was open in the rain, that nobody had closed it—not the wife, not the son—and go inside anyway, exhausted.

All the way up that pastoral highway, Maggie wanted to know all about John Cabot Hamilton. As I was telling her all I knew, as I spoke the words, I realized that I had never pieced together a composite picture of the man. Now that I knew he was an FBI agent, the story became disjointed. The books on his shelf in his study were volumes and volumes of English poetry mixed in with academic tomes on theoretical Marxism and Russian literature. There were three degrees hanging framed on his study walls—Dartmouth, George Washington University and an honorary doctorate from Boston College. He was a scholar. That stuff on those walls did not fit the profile of a director of counterintelligence for the FBI. The way he hunted did fit the profile—follow rules, know your guns. That did make sense, but then a lot of the people up there in the north woods are like that — slow, reserved, understated and careful. Not in any hurry. He liked to tell jokes. I told one to Maggie… a Texas farmer visits a county fair in New Hampshire and gets to talking with a local farmer. The farmer asked the Texan how big his farm was, and the Texan says, "Takes me two days to drive around it," and the local farmer says, "Yup, I had a truck like that once."

"That's funny?"

"Yeah, that's funny but it's also instructional, you know, about character. He was like that. Always instructional. With me, at least."

"What is it about you? Why did he like you so much?"

"I don't know. He had a son and a daughter and there wasn't any tension or bad family stuff that I ever heard, so it wasn't about filling a void or anything. I never met either of them, but it didn't seem like he was looking for something he didn't have. I don't know."

"Why you?"

"Like his note said, 'no one will suspect' me."

"Tobias, it seems to me that he just liked you as a kid, helped you and all that, but then he found something out that might kill him and then, while you were still at Dartmouth, decided to put all his eggs in your basket. His best option."

"Might be, Maggie, might be."

"Tell me another of his jokes."

"Well, this isn't his joke. Bryce told it to me at Dartmouth, but John would have loved it.

"So, there was this writer in New Jersey. But he couldn't write his novel. Too noisy— cars honking, airplanes landing—so he rented a cabin in Pequot Falls and was there, happy as could be—snow falling in quiet woods. Then one evening a knock came at his cabin door. He opened it and there was an old man in overalls. 'Hello, my name is Enoch and I've come to invite you to a party.' 'Sounds great,' the writer said, 'I'd love to come.'

"Well, there might be some dancin'."

"That's okay, I love to dance."

"And there might be some drinkin'."

"Sounds good. I could do with a good shot."

"And there might be some fightin'."

"Used to box in college, not a problem."

"And there might be some sex."

"I'm all in. What should I wear?"

"Oh, come as you are. It's just the two of us."

When Maggie got done laughing and hooting and banging on the dashboard, we were pulling into Pequot Falls. I was tired, ready for bed. Maggie snuggled into me, her head nestled in the crook of my neck. She kissed my chest.

"Who's Bryce? Did he get so smart at Dartmouth like you?"

"I'm not so smart and no, that's where I learned to ski. Bryce taught me."

"Tell me all about it, Tobias, all about it."

8

BY THE TIME I STARTED MY FIRST YEAR at Dartmouth College, I was six feet tall, weighed 255 pounds and wore a size twelve shoe. My Bean Boots had made it only one year, but my mother still kept those boots, my black and red checkered jacket with the burn hole and my itchy wool hat in an upstairs closet at our house in Belmont, Massachusetts. She had been promoted to chief reference librarian at Boston College, eligible for a sabbatical, and was dating a man named Gilbert.

My mother and I went to Pequot Falls every vacation and always for a long hunting weekend. Gilbert never came with us. I spent a lot of time with Mr. Hamilton. When I arrived in Hanover, I had passed my hunter education course, gotten my own adult hunting license and had shot and gutted two bucks—a young six-pointer and an older eight point. I decided to never tell any of my friends at college or in my hometown that I was a hunter and we had a summer house in Pequot Falls. They might think I was rich, which I wasn't, or that I was a murderer of innocent animals, which I was.

Four people wrote me recommendations for my application; the principal of my Belmont school, Chief Stone's wife Isabel, my mother's boss at the library and Mr. Hamilton. I have always believed the reason I got accepted into Dartmouth was the letter from Mr. Hamilton. He was an alumnus. It was beautifully written and said nothing about my scholastic aptitude. All the others talked about how smart I was but, when applying to Dartmouth or any of the other Ivy League schools, that yardstick becomes relative. Only the last few inches matter. I expected to end up at UMASS, if even there. More likely, try it again next year. But Mr. Hamilton's letter quoted Daniel Webster ("There is always room at the top....") and Robert Frost ("Whose woods these are I think I know...."). It was written in a kind of John Wayne vernacular — gritty, hard and you better believe it. He talked about how I was able to overcome obstacles and how I had learned to think critically, make good decisions in difficult situations and learned to always follow through. How I would make a great scholar and citizen. I didn't know any of that about myself. I think to some extent he just made it up. The letter, a copy of which arrived in my mail slot in McLaughlin Hall the day after I arrived, was written on fancy stationary. It was addressed to the Board of Admissions. It was signed:

John Cabot Hamilton
John Cabot Hamilton
Distinguished Fellow, Institute for Global Progress
Dartmouth College class of 1969

A handwritten note, paper-clipped to it, said: *Congratulations, Tobias. 'A+'. Remember the ten rules, they apply everywhere to everything you do. Work hard and stay in touch. Your good friend, John Hamilton.* The envelope it came in was blank—just my name and room number on it—no postage stamp. That's a statement. Someone hand delivered it, either to the college mail room or directly to my little, wooden mail-cubby. He's watching over me, just like when I climbed Black Bear Hill. I realized I had never asked him or my mother what he did for a living. It never occurred to me to ask and nobody ever brought it up. To a teenager, what old people do to make money is not at all important. There it was though—he graduated from Dartmouth and works for a think tank. He was a 'Distinguished Fellow.' That was true. I could vouch for that. For all my years at Dartmouth, that's what I thought.

I knew when I submitted my application to Dartmouth that, if I got in, there was going to be a problem with my attitude concerning skiing and ski resorts. Sneaking peeks at ski bunnies was not on the Big Green program and sharing my true thoughts about the activity would likely get me ostracized if not outright expelled. The captain of the ski team enjoyed the same status on campus as the quarterback of the football team.

All my musing about which sports team to join and the imperative of keeping my mouth shut about skiing would have been fine except for the fact that my roommate, Bryce Haskell, came from a small town in Alabama up by the Tennessee border about ten miles from the only place in that state that has a ski slope. He was the middle child in a family of nine kids from Strupps Corner, Alabama. They were Mormons. His father ran the snow machine and lawn mowers at a ski and golf resort 15 miles away. It snows maybe two inches a month in a hard winter in that part of Alabama, so all the snow on these slopes was manufactured. It was there that Bryce, with free full-time passes, became a first-class skier. Probably the best in all of Alabama. He got so good at it his parents sent him off to live with Mormon friends in the Wasatch Mountains of Utah. He competed in the Giant Slalom at the USSA Junior Regional Championships, got straight 'A's in high school and came to Dartmouth on a full ski-team scholarship. The room was full of skis, snowboards, boots, poles, posters, medals and photographs. It seemed strange for a skier to come from the deep south.

The very first question he asked me was, "Do you ski Cannon or Wildcat?"

The answer I blurted out with no thought behind it at all sealed my fate for the next three years. "I like Mt. Washington."

"Wow!" he said, "an alpine guy. That's totally cool."

No thought behind it at all. For instance, during the winter the average wind speed is 45 mph. 110 days a year there are hurricane force winds up there, usually about twenty feet of snow. The average temperature is somewhere around 8 degrees. 25 people a year have to get saved by Search & Rescue teams from human-triggered avalanches. And there are no ski lifts. You climb for hours up the mountain with your skis on your back, then sidle up to the edge of a cliff, lunge off and slide down a 45 to 60-degree slope into Tuckerman Ravine. I think, without exercising any recommended controls, you could make it from the top of the 'hill' to the bottom in a matter of seconds and then they would find you, still attached to your skis, sometime next July. Wow! An alpine guy. Terrific.

"Where are your skis?"

"Oh, I haven't brought them here yet." Which was true because they were still in a store waiting for me to buy them.

"I've never skied anywhere there aren't lifts."

"Well, I've never skied anywhere there *are* lifts." Technically accurate statement because I'd never skied anywhere at all.

Over the week of orientation, I began to really like my roommate. He was an anomaly, a skier with a southern drawl, but the kind of anomaly that always brings you back a donut and a cup of coffee when he's been out early in the morning. I regretted deceiving him about skiing. It was eating away at me. I began to sense a character flaw—a problem with morality. I was breaking one of Mr. Hamilton's Rules. The growing angst just bounced around in my head, never going anywhere. I needed to talk to somebody.

Ellen Pettigrew, Professor of Government Studies, was also a member of the Dartmouth Ethics Institute. She was a Montana rancher's daughter. It was rumored that she had worked her way through college as a cowgirl in the rodeos before getting her advanced degrees from Georgetown and Harvard. She was tall, had long silver hair pinned back with turquoise clasps and a voice as soft as snow.

She motioned me to a chair in her office. I laid out all the circumstances of my problem, word for word as best I could, concluding with my fear that it was a fundamental defect in my moral fiber. She didn't say I had a problem. She didn't say I might talk to a psychologist about this. She asked me what professional path I might want to pursue.

"I think I want to be a journalist."

"Then we'll attack this issue from that perspective."

She re-stated that everything I had said was factually true, so the problem is the notion that an implied truth which is not a truth is disturbing but less egregious than a lie. From a journalistic point of view, that is wrong. Using out-of-place, out-of-context facts to lead a reader to believe something you know to be untrue is just as bad as an outright lie. It may be worse. Purposely misusing facts to create an alternative truth which isn't true at all is an evil breach of trust between you and your listener or your reader.

"However, if you had said you wanted to be a politician, I would recommend you carry on with your deceptions. Hone them to a sharp blade. That 'character flaw' you're worried about is a politician's stock-in-trade. But if you want to be a respected journalist, start your rehabilitation by truthfully discussing it with your roommate. Watch out for any other instances and immediately correct them." Then she asked a most curious question. "If you count an elephant's trunk as a leg, how many legs does an elephant have?"

"Five?"

"No, calling an elephant's trunk a leg doesn't make it a leg. That's a politician's trick. Elephants have four legs. The truth is the truth. Always. Don't try to change it. Let me know how your conversation with your roommate goes. Truly, let me know. I'm interested and, Tobias, there's nothing wrong with you or you wouldn't have chosen to come here to see me. I suggest you take one of the classes in religion. That's where the issue of ethics begins. It's also where, from a journalist's world view, most of the conflicts begin. Don't forget to confess to Bryce." She knew who he was. She had done her homework. On my way out, she stopped me. "Do you know John Hamilton?

"Yes, yes I do. He's a good friend of mine. He taught me to hunt. Do you know him?"

"I do. He's a very good and very smart man. You couldn't have a better teacher."

"Yeah, he sure is. He's a Distinguished Fellow at a think tank."

She waited a small moment, then said, "Yes, he is that."

So, I confessed. Bryce told me he'd already figured out I wasn't an alpine skier because he had left an article on the dresser titled *The World's Most Dangerous Mountains,* and I had never mentioned it. Mt. Washington was #8, right after Everest. He'd figured anybody who liked to ski there was either mentally deranged or dead and, since I wasn't either of those, I must have liked the mountain for some other reason. I had read the article and had come to the same conclusion, so I decided not to even bring it up again. He asked me if I was interested in learning to ski and I said yes. His tutelage began right there with a series of squatting exercises intended to strengthen my leg muscles. He promised me that I'd be doing the downhill slalom by springtime snowmelt.

An April snow was already a foot deep and falling fast with fat flakes. As I pulled up to the house, I could see the hump of the stump at the back of the field.

"How's your toaster doing, Mr. Hamilton?"

"Dead. Goddamn thing."

"I'm surprised your wife lets you leave it out there."

"It's my field, besides, there are a lot of good memories out on that stump. That's where you learned to shoot."

"Yeah, I remember. Someday, when your wife gets tired of looking at it, I'd love to have it. I'd put it on a nice base and call it my first real sculpture. A true work of art. Not now, but someday after I grow up and have someplace to put it."

"Just let me know when you've grown up—it will be yours that very day."

That simple notion, that I should let him know when I'm grown up, conveyed such a strong trust in me. Usually, one would say, 'Mr. Carter's boy is all grown up,' meaning, maybe, nothing more than he was big now and had a job. This was different. Mr. Hamilton wasn't going to make that determination, I was. It was up to me to know when I had left behind the trappings of youth. All his work with me—the rifles, hunting, woodsmanship and honesty—all came from that singular notion—trust yourself.

"You know, I've never told anybody at college that I go deer hunting every year. I don't know why, but I feel like it's better left alone."

"I never did either. It is kind of a private thing and most Dartmouth students wouldn't understand the universality of it. Can you get some wood from the porch? Let's light a fire in the den and catch up."

"Universality?"

"Get some wood. Say hi to Jane on your way. She's in the kitchen with Isabel."

Bryce was up at Cannon Mountain skiing with his friends from the team until the slopes closed. They all were going to stay in a motel, then Bryce was going to pick me up at Mr. Hamilton's house early in the morning and we would to drive back to school on Sunday.

Bryce had given me my ski lesson that morning. I was getting to the point of not needing lessons anymore. I wouldn't say I was an expert, but I could fly past almost everybody on the intermediate slopes, only falling when I forgot Rule #5 (*Always Be Aware of Your Surroundings*) and would hit a patch of moguls going way too fast. I hadn't broken any bones yet but twice the ski patrol had given me a lift down the hill on their sled. Just to be safe, they said. Just to get me out of there before I killed somebody was more like it. Bryce had said that he would continue teaching me until I could beat him down the black diamond Tramline trail. That was not likely to ever happen. Bryce didn't fall.

There is nothing sweeter than an apple wood fire in a stone fireplace on a snowy evening, watching the flakes build up on the windowsill, talking with a good friend, sipping a snifter of brandy. The fire burns orange-bright and smells like Thanksgiving. Talk is always slow, measured, metronomic, paced to the crack and snap of the wood with long breaks between words to watch the flames. Life doesn't get much better than that.

I pointed out the window. In the field was a grey lynx in the snow. It looked like an adult, maybe two feet tall at the shoulder, tufted ears with black tips, leaping one bound at a time through the deepening snow, pausing, leaping again. It was a beautiful sight—ears twitching, nose pointed up, sniffing, soft spotted fur against the whiteness of the snowy evening. The first forage of the night, perhaps following a rabbit.

"Lynx are very rare here. Don't see them often," he said, his chin in his hand, looking out.

"Lynxe," I said. "That was the name of that girl at the party I told you about. Where the boy got his leg chopped off. Mary Sue Lynxe. She was a lot like that—beautiful, rare and predatory. Somebody told me she died up in Canada. Got shot somehow."

"May Sue Lynxe. Fascinating name. Brings up images. Lynx is a special beast in many cultures. The Native Americans call them the *keeper of secrets*. Tell me again about that night in the woods and all those young people. It's intriguing how that happens." I started the story at a dead deer registration and ended it with a newspaper article that came out the next day. Then we sat in silence, ingesting it all.

"My God," I said, "it's so quiet."

He smiled. "Look for what isn't there. Listen for the noise that went away. That's where the truth hides." The lynx was gone.

"Tobias, since I'm an alumnus, I get *The Dartmouth* every month. I've been following your articles on the presidential campaigns. They're good, very well researched, but you're missing an important component."

"What is that?"

"You seem to convey that what Donald Trump says is what he thinks. That is not at all true. Those two things are completely unrelated to each other. There is no credible evidence that Trump believes in anything. Except himself and his money. He might just win the presidency. That's how deep the distrust of Hilary Clinton runs in this country. She is the poster child for everything wrong with Washington. But Trump can't get there without some very powerful people helping. You won't see them or hear them. I'm not talking about politicians or big money people. We can see all those guys. It's the dark money and the foreign actors that are invisible to the public eye. You'll find their tracks in the snow or hear the sound that used to be there. That's it, nothing more. That's the only way to find them."

"Where do I start?"

"Your esteemed advisor, Ms. Ellen Pettigrew, and I have jointly nominated you for a seat in a very select and advanced journalism program. Only ten students from around the country, all seniors. It is taught by a professor from Harvard. It happens to be in New Hampshire this year. Interestingly, it's going to be in a house once lived in by Madam Chiang-Kai-Shek when she and her husband were fleeing China. It's on Lake Winnipesaukee. It's part of a program called the Gemma Institute. Dr. Alice Turnbell, a super-star in the world of forensic linguistics, teaches it. How to understand what people really mean by knowing where they come from and what words, idioms and vernaculars they use. She also teaches at Langley, training people to be the best spies in the world. You're going to enjoy it, m'boy. She's smart and tough as rawhide."

They had just nominated me. Filled out an application, put my name all over it, attached some papers to it and sent it off to a review committee. There were probably dozens of them.

"How do you know I'm going to get in?"

"Ms. Pettigrew is a renowned professor and, quite humbly, they are very familiar with me and my work. They look for people who can hunt in the woods alone and ski off the edge of 50-degree precipice without shitting their pants. You will receive an invitation. Just say yes."

"I haven't pushed off the brink of Tuckerman Ravine yet. I don't know if I'd shit my pants."

"I know that. That's why I asked you to come up here today. So, I wouldn't be a liar. How about we go tomorrow morning bright and early. Your ski team buddy will be here. He'll love it. It's supposed to be a fine day."

9

IT WAS A FINE DAY, UNTIL IT WASN'T. That's Mt. Washington. Mr. Hamilton, Bryce and I arrived at the Pinkham Notch Trailhead camp at eight in the morning. We waited in the entry drive while a bus finished unloading passengers from Boston — city skiers. It was April warm and the sky was bright and cloudless.

Mr. Hamilton pointed to the top of the mountain. "It's four miles up there and more than 3000' vertical from here with your skis on your back. You in?"

"Yes sir," we both said.

"Short story. The first people to ski that bowl up there were Dartmouth skiers. Then years later, in 1939, a kid named Toni Matt was racing a Dartmouth guy named Dick Durance. Matt misjudged the edge of the lip, went right over it full bore and couldn't christie. Couldn't dig in sideways to slow down. He came straight down the headwall in a schuss. Bullet-like crouch, poles tucked under his armpits. He made it from up there to right here in six and a half minutes. Four miles. At times he was going 90 miles an hour. Couldn't stand up to slow down. That was seventy-eight years ago and nobody, nobody has ever even come close to breaking that record. Well, truth be told, there have been some races — they call it the American Inferno, but there are no records of anybody even trying to beat six minutes — it's a suicide mission."

Bryce said, "A lot of guys out in Utah talked about that run. It's legendary, all over the world." I remembered him telling me that anybody who wanted to ski this mountain was either deranged or dead. That must have been where it came from.

Sunday in early April and lots of people were setting out up the mountain path. We waited for a long break so that we could climb alone, so that we could be in among the Balsam Fir where the only sound was the crunching of our boots on the snow. The night freeze had crusted the top but the hikers before us had broken a clean path and knocked clear the snow laden boughs. We didn't talk. There was nothing to say.

For two hours we climbed that route, steeper and steeper. The trees became gnarled and bent by the wind, shorter, their growth stunted by the cold and an ever-decreasing season of snow-free days. When we reached the Rangers' camp at the base of the ravine, the first clouds came over the mountain top, the wind picked up and the summit disappeared in a fog. Mr. Hamilton knew both Park Rangers at the camp and they traded stories about the mountain, about all the uncertainties, then talked about the dangers there were now that concealed-carry weapons on federal park land were allowed. These Rangers had tried to get at least an exemption for this mountain because of the likelihood of triggering an avalanche but nobody in Washington wanted to hear it.

"About a month ago, one guy went into a major wipe out near the lip, fell two hundred feet with a loaded 9MM Glock in his backpack. He'd just stuffed it in there with a bunch of other things, like cramp-ons. Guess what? The safety was off — it blew a hole right through his liver. Dead before we got to him. Seen people do a lot of dumb things up on this mountain, but that's gotta get the blue ribbon for stupid."

"No," Mr. Hamilton said, "the blue ribbon goes to Capitol Hill and the NRA. That guy just gets the consolation prize — a free trip to the morgue. A lot of that going around."

It looked like the weather had started turning bad, so we hiked our way across the bottom of the bowl to a pathway that lead up 1000' to the rim of the ravine. Grasping rocks for handholds and kicking in footholds with our boots, we climbed ever slower and slower as the grade steepened to more than 45 degrees. I was in the middle. Mr. Hamilton was in the lead. For a man of seventy or so, he was nimble and sure. He'd been here before. He knew it could be done. I didn't know that. Not at all. Bryce was behind but, as I struggled to get my fingers in some kind of crease in a roundish rock, he passed me. I wanted to yell out no! don't leave me in the rear, what if I slip, what if I fall and slide to the bottom? I want you behind me! But I just grunted and tried to keep up.

The wind was quickening, blowing down the bowl, across my face, and the fog had thickened, rolling over the lip. I could see Bryce, but I'd lost Mr. Hamilton. He must be near the top. *Always Know Where You Are and How to Get Back to Where You Came From.* Well, that shouldn't be hard. Just let go and in a jiffy, I'd be down at the bottom, maybe dead. *Don't Panic.* Okay, okay, just keep climbing, follow Bryce. Dig in. Get there.

The lip came in sight. Mr. Hamilton reached out a hand and pulled me up and over. "We made it." He looked me in the eyes, both hands on my shoulders and nodded his head. "At the end of every path, one danger is behind and another is ahead."

He pointed to rocky out-cropping. "See that scarp? When I was younger, I would climb up here alone, sit on those rocks, and, before I descended, I would leave all my thoughts in those granite crevices."

There we were, on top of the headwall on Mt. Washington, staring down Tuckerman Ravine. Far, far down the mountain, four miles away, three thousand feet down, I could just make out smoke rising from the stone chimney of the base camp. Six minutes? That guy made it from here to there in six minutes? Incredible. Frightening. I peered over the edge and it seemed to drop straight down. Like almost vertical for a thousand feet ending in a field of rocks. Jesus, Mary and Joseph. Don't panic. Don't shit your pants.

Mr. Hamilton said if he was going to make good on his statement to the Gemma people, whoever they were, we would have to go over the Ice Fall. It was the steepest descent but the only one that would truly qualify me as a fearless conqueror of adversity. Any shallower slope might leave niggling questions. Questions aren't good.

"I'm going first. Tobias, you come next and Bryce, can you bring up the rear to make sure we all get there? Watch me. Remember you must brake, dig in your edges, slow down, get in control before you jump the lip. Be Aware of Your Surroundings and Keep Your Skis Pointed in A Safe Direction—not straight down. See you at the bottom." The old man pushed off and christied side to side four or five times before he vanished from sight.

The wind bit at my cheeks as I wiped the fog from my goggles. "Okay, Alpine guy, this is what it's all about, right? This is the whole deal." Bryce gave me a quick clumsy hug and a soft pat on the shoulder. "Rip it!" I smiled and nodded, looked down the slope, took a deep breath and pushed off.

I don't remember concentrating, planning, scanning the hill, calculating. I don't remember pushing hard on my poles or digging in my edges on a turn. I didn't hear the air ripping past my ears or feel the waxed skis slapping the ice lumps. I don't remember hearing, feeling, thinking or doing anything at all. When my body stopped and came to rest, it was as though I had spent a year at a Buddhist retreat staring at a blank wall. I was washed clean, my soul scrubbed. I stood still, immobile, except for the slightest shiver of pure joy.

I was notified of my acceptance into the Gemma program by a shriek and a hug. I was in Ms. Pettigrew's last class of the year when a graduate student came in and whispered in her ear. She let out a yelp and came through the crowded classroom and wrapped her arms around me, right in front of everybody.

"Students, Tobias has been accepted into the prestigious Gemma Institute Program. The first Dartmouth graduate ever to be awarded this coveted fellowship. Only ten last-semester seniors from around the country are admitted each year. What an honor. What an honor for Tobias and for our school. Let's give him a hand." Everybody clapped and I was more embarrassed than I'd ever been.

The first night there, we were all shown our rooms. Chloe, Dr. Turnbell's teaching assistant, went from room to room, sitting on the edge of the bed and asking how everything was. Was there anything she could do to make our fellowship week more comfortable or rewarding? I doubt anyone said there was anything more she should do. It all seemed perfect. Her eyes were hazel green and her voice was bel canto. She was so comforting, like a goodnight kiss.

Dr. Turnbell described the power of words without image, of hearing without seeing and how the intonation of voice and accent in phone conversations, radio broadcasts, tape recordings and interrogations is so powerful that it can easily mislead the listener. How dangerous it is to be sure you're hearing something that isn't in the words. Chloe helped with this presentation by dividing us into two groups: half in one room, half in another. In one room, all the windows were blacked out with thick drapes and the lights shut off. It was pitch dark. I was in there. The woman—I assumed it was a woman because of her voice—told a ten-minute story about her life. She was one of twelve children who grew up in a small, rural town. They were poor. It was a simple story. She spoke with that distinctive accent of northern Wisconsin. Almost Canadian. We were asked to leave the room, let the other group come in, and write all our thoughts about what kind of childhood this must have been.

When the next group was assembled in the blackness, the woman spoke again. None of us had seen her. She told exactly the same story, word for word. Then, that group was left to go write their impressions of her childhood. The results were amazing—two completely different childhoods. The second story had been told in a deep southern drawl, like Mississippi or Alabama. Most of the Wisconsin stories were with snow and lakes. A healthy, happy family, albeit poor. The Mississippi stories were about heat and flat landscapes, cotton, real poverty and poor education. The stuff of stereotypes. When the lights came on, she was a short black woman with wavy grey hair, big glasses and a hard-set jaw. Born and raised in Los Angeles, a teacher of spies. The host of a weekly show on WBUR radio in Boston called, *She Said, He Said.*

Another one of the days was spent talking about false conclusions that come from your mind cross-associating things you've seen that may be factually unrelated to the circumstance.

A man wants to give you a tip on a terrorist plot to blow up a synagogue in the Bronx. You meet him in a Syrian restaurant in a Muslim neighborhood. He has a full beard and is wearing a taqiyah, like every other man in the restaurant. You take his tip seriously—he should know. When the synagogue is blown up, it turns out it was by a domestic Neo-Nazi group. The man you talked to masterminded the attack. He was neither Middle-Eastern nor a Muslim. He just wanted you to think he was to throw off your investigation. It worked.

We would leave in the morning. Chloe came in and sat at the foot of my bed. She was holding an envelope. It was a letter from the *Boston Globe*. They were offering me a job starting on Monday morning. I just stared at Chloe.

"You've made a good impression here. And it helps to have connected friends." She hugged me and left.

10

HE HAD IMPLORED ME TO FIND HIS FILES and then abruptly died. If that death was accidental, his files were still important. If he had been murdered because of them, they may be more than important, they might be vital to the nation. I had to figure that out before I could know how much risk I was willing to take on—for me, for Maggie and maybe a lot of other innocent people.

A faint crimson stain of his blood was still on the ground a month after John Hamilton was shot. He had said, *follow my path to the end,* and it looked like this was the end of his path. Blood stains in a field. Nothing more. Tire tracks of what I assumed were ambulances and police cars were still visible in the tall grass. The field was wide open from the wood line on the east where the blood was, all the way up to thick pines on the west. There was a three-foot-high ridge about thirty feet from the blood. Everyone in town knew what had happened and knew where and when it happened. Beanie Weeks, a one-legged guy, about my age, sitting on a stool behind the cash register at the country store, told me all about it.

"That story is bullshit. Didn't happen that way. Tom Duncan don't mistake a man for a deer and shoot it. He just don't. I don't care if it was a drizzly, bad day, Tom Duncan can tell a man from a deer in the middle of the night. And he had a goddamn scope. Double don't. Something else happened and ain't nobody around here wants to talk about it."

That wasn't true. A lot of people wanted to talk about it and everyone I spoke with had the same reservations about the story. Some, like Beanie, because Tom Duncan wouldn't make a mistake. "That's a Massachusetts mistake. Local hunters don't make that mistake. Especially Tom Duncan."

Others, like the gas station attendant, because John Hamilton was a serious FBI man who was about to spill the beans on Donald Trump in a secret meeting. "No wonder they shot his ass. Simple as that."

The *New York Times* had published their article. There probably hadn't been a *New York Times* sold in this town in its two-hundred-year history, but today, there were copies on the store counters, on the front seats of parked cars, even at the town hall. They were all over the place. The article didn't say much, mostly talked about John Hamilton, his life, his death and his serious disagreements with power brokers in Washington. They had gotten statements from three people—Tom Duncan, the Fish & Game officer and the county attorney. The statements were printed but no truth emerged that bound them together. They were, it seemed to me, contradictory to the storyline of the whole incident. It was clear that none of the law enforcement people in the north country had given the *Times* reporters any official documents at all, just random words. That didn't bode well for me, but more than a month had passed since the shooting.

I drove by the Presidential Inn. The whole of the Presidential Range stretched across the horizon. Sitting in a rocking chair on the front porch was a very distinguished looking white-haired gentleman who looked like he knew a lot about a lot of things. He also looked familiar. I couldn't place him. It might have been from the newspapers or magazines. I parked, walked up the wide stairs and plunked down in a rocking chair beside him.

"Well good morning, young man. How is this fine day treating you?"

It dawned on me who he was. I'd seen him on TV a dozen times. The flowing hair, the suspenders, the southern drawl were a dead give-away. J. William Conklin, the famed civil rights attorney.

"Thank you, Mr. Conklin, I'm doing very well. Sir, do you happen to be here because of the shooting death of John Hamilton?"

"Oh, no, no, oh gracious me, no. I'm on a small vacation from the rigors of battling with the President of the United States. It's enough to wear a good man out." He pronounced it, 'rigas' and 'YOO-nited. "And you? Not the view, I suspect."

"I'm sorry, sir. My name is Tobias Starkey and I'm a reporter for the *Boston Globe*. As I was passing by, I thought I recognized you and thought maybe you were here for the same reason I am. That's all. I just wanted to find out if you knew anything I didn't know about Mr. Hamilton's death."

"Well, I don't know what you know, but I don't know much about it at all. I have been told that the young man who said he shot him had been charged with 'negligently shooting a human being while hunting,' pled *nolo contendere* in court, was fined five hundred dollars and had his hunting license suspended for ten years. That much I do know. I heard that not more than twenty minutes ago. The case was closed. I do have a few observations that I derive from knowing who Hamilton is, or was, I should say."

"Yes?"

"I am not suggesting that murder took place in this fine town, but simply that there is sufficient smoke to indicate it might have. I have no smoking gun, but in my heart, I think Hamilton was murdered. I'm not so sure that young fellow Duncan did it, but, bear this mind as you poke around, there was never more of a motive to kill a man."

A woman came onto the porch and said, "J.W., your breakfast is hot and ready, just how you like it."

He put his hand on my shoulder. "Dig, boy, dig. Dig 'till you hit pay dirt. Then come on down to Washington and knock on my door. Corner of 1st and D. Conklin Kennedy. I'll be there." He hefted his rotund frame up, snapped his suspenders, and followed the woman into the hotel. I wrote it down in my steno pad.

The case was closed. So, said the legal giant. All documents in the public domain should be available. Should be. I decided to try Chief Stone first—he should have them all and he knew me. I also decided to take Maggie with me. She was like Jasmine — people liked her, they went on and on about things they shouldn't talk about. She smiles pretty-like and nudges their stories out. She grew up with cops all around.

I had never been to Chief Stone's house, even though it was no more than a ten-minute walk from my house or Mr. Hamilton's house. His car was there. I've always thought a police chief's yard would be clean and tidy, above average, and project an image of solid Americana. A flag on a pole, neatly mowed lawns, edged walkways, BBQ grill covered with its fitted black tarp, siding and window shutters painted, cars washed and parked in such a way they could quickly exit the drive. Everything ship-shape so people could trust that everything they did would also be ship-shape. Not so with Chief Stone.

The town cruiser was muddy and pulled in tight between a backhoe with no bucket, its empty knuckle in the dirt, and a big black box sitting on the ground that looked like a horse trailer with no wheels. The cruiser door could only open wide enough to allow a person to slither in as long as their gun and holster didn't get hung up on the door jamb. But Chief Stone was a skinny man, maybe he could slide in. He didn't need a lawnmower — there wasn't any lawn, just weeds. A front porch had been under construction for the last ten years or so. The wood had weathered grey. It was cordoned off by plastic tape hanging limp in the still morning air — POLICE LINE — DO NOT CROSS. The entry door was around the side and seemed to lead into a basement. He was a friend of John Hamilton and so was I. That, at least, ought to open up a good conversation. It didn't.

Isabel Stone opened the door and put her hands on my shoulders. "My, my, Tobias Starkey, haven't you grown up. A Dartmouth graduate and a fine-looking young man. Come in, come in, come in. Who is this lovely girl with you?"

"Mrs. Stone, this is a friend of mine from Boston, Maggie James."

"Please come in, it is so good to see you, Tobias. Would you like a cup of coffee?" Maggie instantly said yes, we would both love a cup of coffee. The door did lead into a basement, but it was a basement that was also the living room. Sofas, chairs, TV, bookshelves and a gun cabinet. There were windows, but they were all four feet off the floor. They were high up and there was no other door out of the space. A staircase in the corner led up to what must have been the kitchen, dining room, bathrooms and bedrooms because there was none of that down there. Chief Stone was sitting on the sofa. He didn't get up.

"Well, Tobias, I hear you're a reporter now. *Boston Globe*, if I recall it right. What brings you back to this part of the world? Are you paying your respects to John or are you looking for a story?"

I don't know how he knew about me but there it was. All of it. Just as stark and plain as Ellen Pettigrew could have framed it. The truth is the truth. Period. Just as clear as Mr. Hamilton made it — fishermen lie, hunters don't. Looking at this policeman, sitting down, in uniform with his gun and badges, knobby fingers on his knees, his grey and narrow face, lips flat, unexpressive, and puffy eyes wandering all over my face, I remembered something else Mr. Hamilton told me — don't wear any visible white, don't be the deer the hunter wants to shoot.

"I'm not looking for a story, Chief Stone, I just want to know how it happened, so I can..."

He interrupted me. "Tom Duncan thought John Hamilton was a deer and he shot him. It's hunting season. Unfortunately, that happens sometimes. There's nothing more to it."

"Mrs. Hamilton told me that you and Jim Lacey were going out with him, but he was alone, wasn't he.? How did that happen?"

He was silent for a long time. I thought he was weighing his options — answer the question, tell me get out or shoot me. "She's right about that, we were all going to hook up, but at nine in the morning, not six. I don't know where she got that damn fool notion we were going out at six. We weren't."

I likewise looked at my options. Tell him that's a bullshit answer because everybody knows most bucks are gone by nine in the morning, keep pushing and ask him where Jim Lacey was or see if he would give me the official reports, which is what I came for in the first place. "Agent Lacey must also have thought it was supposed to be at nine because he didn't show up either. Mr. Hamilton must have got it wrong."

"Looks as though he got it dead wrong. Jim Lacey was out hunting on the other side of the mountain."

"Does that mean…"

He interrupted me again. "I got a busy day ahead and I need to get on with it." He yelled up the stairs to the kitchen where his wife and Maggie had gone. "Isabel, cancel that coffee order. These two young folks need to be going now."

"Chief Stone, can you at least give me copies of the official reports, so I can put this to rest in my head?"

"No. I don't have them. I recused myself. Friend of the family. The State Police have them. They're at headquarters, all the way down in Concord. I got a piece of advice for you: put this to rest right now. Today. You're barking up an empty tree. There ain't no possum in those branches. It's sad this happened but that's how it is…Isabel!!!"

Maggie and I sat on the front porch beside my father's flag, drinking hot chocolate with whipped cream and talking it all over. A perfect noontime break. At sunset, yesterday, it was the same but with a glass of brandy in a snifter. Maggie was really impressed that I had, serendipitously, run into one of the great legal minds, Mr. J. William Conklin, ESQ. I was equally impressed that she had chatted it up with Isabel Stone and found out that her husband was seriously disturbed by the whole event. She said he wasn't himself these days. Maybe it was the whiskey he and Jim Lacey had drunk that night before Mr. Hamilton got shot, enough so Stone had slept late, and Lacey couldn't go home even though his house was in the same town. He'd slept overnight on the sofa. That didn't make sense. If Lacey had gone off hunting early on the other side of the mountain, how did Chief Stone, if he was asleep, know that and where did Lacey get his rifle, ammo, and hunting clothes? Did he drive home early, get all his stuff, pound down coffee and then trudge off to go hunting all by himself at 6AM when he (apparently) thought the three of them were going out at 9AM? Was he going to go out hunting twice?

To me, at least, on the phone two weeks ago, Jane Hamilton had been very certain of the plan that they all go hunting together at 6AM. I wasn't at all sure there wasn't a possum up in that tree somewhere. Maggie wasn't all that sure that there is nothing unusual about people getting shot to death during hunting season. It was clear we wouldn't learn any more except gossip from the local folk. We needed to go to Concord.

"Tobias, I thought this was a Fish & Game issue, that they were in charge and the case was closed. Why are the records at the State Police?"

"No idea. Let's go find out."

Most state offices are in a large government complex a few miles from downtown Concord, the New Hampshire state capital. We drove around and found the State Police headquarters as well as Fish & Game. Better to ask Fish & Game first and find out if they have the records and, if they don't, why not? The woman at the front desk heard our question and immediately sprung from her seat and disappeared into a warren of offices. She was gone for five minutes and, I think, was surprised to find us still standing there when she came back from her extended conferences.

"This department has no records of that event. I'm very sorry."

"What department does have those records? I mean, it did happen. A man was killed in a hunting accident, so somebody has the records. Who would that be? I mean normally that would be you, wouldn't it?"

She disappeared again. This time she wasn't gone as long but she was clearly getting a bit frazzled.

"Who are you? Can I see some identification?"

This time Maggie spoke up. "No, it's none of your business who we are if you don't have any intention of giving us records. Tell your boss or whoever is hiding back there that we will file a Freedom of Information Act request and then you'll know who we are. Just like the law says." She took my hand, turned and pushed open the exit door. No goodbye, no thank you, nothing, just left.

The State Police were no better. Same routine. Maggie asked if that woman at Fish & Game had called ahead warning them of our impending arrival and she said, "No," as she nodded her head. Maggie, mimicking her head-nod, asked her which it was, yes or no?

The woman said, "You have to leave now."

I sensed that Maggie was about to lunge over the counter and rip her Adam's Apple out, so I took her arm and tugged her out into the parking lot and got her in the car.

"Maggie, don't piss them off. That's dangerous."

"I am not one bit afraid of cops. Period. Not one bit."

"I am."

"Well, get over it. If they see you're afraid of them, they will fuck with you and never give you a single piece of paper. And then they'll jerk you around some more just for the fun of it because they know they can. Not giving us one document, which by the way, is public information, is like hanging out a banner that says, *Something Is Really Fucked Up Around Here!!!* In the morning, I'm calling

87

Daddy. We'll see how they like that. What a bunch of shitheads. Stupid, too. Stupid shitheads. They shouldn't have done that. Now we're going to fuck with them."

She called Daddy in the morning before he went to the bar. She didn't have a mother. Her mother had died of cancer when she was eight and Johnny James had raised her alone. He had quit his job as a security consultant, resigned from the police commission and opened his bar. He sat Maggie on a bar stool every day after school and he watched over his only cub like a lion. She'd do her homework and when the night-shift bartender came on at six, he'd take her home and cook dinner. They weren't just close, they were almost one thing. Getting between them was very dangerous.

She told him everything we had learned and all about our trip to Concord.

"Gosh, Daddy, you wouldn't believe how rude those people were. It was scary." Daddy didn't like people being rude to his daughter. He didn't like that at all.

"He wants to talk to you." She handed me the phone.

His voice was morning gravely. "Maggie said there's a guy named Jim Lacey involved in this thing. Is that right?" I said it was. "He was a lieutenant on the Boston PD, a real up-and-comer before the FBI snatched him away. You listen to me. You be real careful around that guy and I men real careful. Do you understand what I'm saying?"

"Yes, sir, I do."

"Good. Give me back to my daughter."

"Daddy, what does this Jim Lacey guy look like so if we see him we will know to stay clear? ... Yes, uh huh, that tall? ... A limp? Wow! Okay, thanks Daddy."

Two days later, at noon while we were sipping our hot chocolate on the porch, a white sedan parked in the driveway. It had government tags and the seal of the State of New Hampshire on the car doors. A lanky black- haired man in a sharp suit and tie came up the steps. He was carrying a thick manila envelope.

"Miss James, if I'm not mistaken? My, how you've grown up. I used to help you with your homework. I'm Al Tortelli." He held out his hand for shaking and Maggie took it in both her hands.

"Of course I remember you. You were a big help, I never could figure out those math problems. Please, Mr. Tortelli, please sit down. This is my friend, Tobias Starkey. He is an investigative reporter for the *Boston Globe.*"

"Yes," he said shaking my hand, "so I've been told."

He sat.

"Maggie, this is for you," he said handing her the envelope. "There's something you should know before diving into the documents. New Hampshire has a Right to Know law that is much quicker in response than the federal Freedom of Information Act. But it's somewhat less expansive. Certain documents can't be released because you're neither a family member nor an attorney representing the family. That would include photos of the deceased and the autopsy and ballistics reports. Those aren't here. But an FOI request might have taken months, maybe longer, maybe even a court hearing because," he took his time, looking at me, "there are people who believe this incident to be, quite simply, an unfortunate hunting accident and any attempt to make it look like something else would be politically motivated—nothing more."

"Would that include your boss, the Attorney General?"

"Yes, Maggie, it would. I wouldn't be here with this information if my boss hadn't personally gotten a call from the Suffolk County

DA. He didn't like it, but I think he's okay with it now. Given the public information laws, somebody would have eventually gotten here." He turned to me again. "We concluded it was better to give this to you than almost anyone else. You're young and a friend of Mr. Hamilton. That makes political motivation an unlikely driver. Am I right about that?"

"Yes."

"A downside is also that you're young. Your boss at the *Globe*, whoever that is, may push you to do and say things you shouldn't do or say. Is that a problem?"

"No sir, it isn't. I only have a boss if he doesn't do that. If he does, I'll walk away."

Al Toretelli stood and smiled, patted me on the shoulder and said, "Maggie, this is in your name. Could you sign this? It's an information request. It's all filled out, just needs your signature for my files." She signed it. "This is important for both of you: be fair, open-minded and careful; you don't want to hurt anybody. Remember, almost everyone involved in this knew John Hamilton. That includes the shooter. These small towns are pretty tight knit. Say hello to your father."

11

THERE WERE 12 BLACK AND WHITE GLOSSY PHOTOGRAPHS, 64 pages of documents, 14 of which were radio, telephone and daily status logs for all of State Police Troop F activities for November 9. That's a log of everything any officer or dispatch person did or said over a 2,000 square mile area for 24 hours. Interesting—man left dog/cat in car 3 days at Hogback and—juvenile suspect shot woman's garbage can many times, garbage all over the place. A lot of them went like this: Conway ref F&G 222 10-9 356 5128 ref wound deer on airport runway 222 OK. Interesting but not so helpful. The deer escaped. We separated those out, leaving 38 pages.

"Draw straws," said Maggie.

"Why?"

"Good guy, bad guy. We both read each document, the good guy, long straw, gets to say why the statements are logical and justified. Bad guy, short straw, says why it doesn't make sense or contradicts something else." She gave me the arched eyebrow look. She held out her hand with two matches cupped in her fingers, only the heads poking out. I got the bad guy. We cleared off a whole wall on the screened-in porch and push-pinned all documents up in chronological order, starting with the statements made by Tom Duncan, Chief Stone, Fish & Game officers and State Policemen at the scene, then the accident investigation reports. Across the bottom were a dozen letters of correspondence and a map of Pequot Falls showing the shooting site, the police chief's house and John Hamilton's house. I put the map, photographs, a magnifying glass and two pads of paper on a small table. Ready.

Tom Duncan had given his statement, in his own writing, to a Fish & Game officer after having been read his Miranda rights.

I woke up at approximately 4:30. At 5:00 I went to pick up a friend. The friend was not up. I waited 15 minutes until 5:15 or so. I drove to the Chesterfield home and drove up the old Range Road and back down to the Chesterfield home. I walked out to the place where I was going to sit, shined my flashlight around the field and sat down backed into the woods. I sat until approximately 6:10 when I stood up to go pick up a friend and saw a motion on the other side of the field. I picked up my rifle and through the scope I saw brown. I dropped my rifle down and saw a flicker of white. I'm not sure what it was but thought it was the flag of a deer. At this time when I saw the white it appeared to move a little faster and I thought it had smelled me and was now running. I picked up my rifle and through the scope saw brown again and squeezed the trigger. I put my flashlight and hot seat down in a well house and walked towards the deer which I thought I had missed. I was about 50 yards away when I saw white and thought it was a deer. I got about 25 yards away and saw a man lying there. I went to him and dragged him out of the woods and started Cardio Pulmonary Resuscitation when I saw the bullet wound. I tried to carry him to the road but he was too heavy so I put him down and ran to my Scout and drove to Chief Stone's home. I got him out of bed. He made the necessary phone calls.

"Well, that's pretty straightforward. That's what happened. His friend wasn't awake, so he went hunting alone. He saw something move, saw brown and saw white and he shot, walked down there and saw a dead man lying on the ground. He tried to resuscitate him, couldn't, so he tried to carry him to get to a hospital, but he was too heavy, so he drove to the Chief of Police's house and woke him up."

"Yeah, Maggie, that is the gist of it, but how long had he been sitting there before he stood up to get a friend (he didn't say it was the same friend) and saw motion, saw brown, saw white. That's important because John Hamilton had to get there somehow, so why didn't he see him walking across the field to get to where he was shot?"

"He said he dragged him out of the woods. He was in the woods, not the field."

"We'll, I don't know about that. Look at this photo. It shows two rifles, a hat and blood on the ground. It's clearly in the field, not in the woods. If Duncan dragged him out of the woods, how did Hamilton's gun get there, lying right beside his own. He certainly wouldn't have dragged Hamilton's gun along with the body. Why would he try that? And, why would he, the 26-year-old son of a State Trooper, try CPR (weirdly spelling the whole thing out) before finding out what the problem was? Why would anyone drag a person if they don't have a clue what's wrong with them? Maybe they have a broken neck or a coronary occlusion. What? Did he drag him by his head? Arms? Feet? Those are strange things to do. Drag a person 15 feet through the woods, like bump, bump, bump, then start CPR. Did he think it was a heart attack? And then see a bullet wound? Ooopsy, Poopsy, Mr. Hamilton, sorry about that. Where was this bullet wound?"

I scanned the photos and two were of the jacket that John had been wearing. One showed the entry wound and the other showed the exit wound. He was shot in the back. The bullet went in about the middle of his shoulder blade on the right side and came out above the collar bone on the left side of his neck. He would have been walking away from the shooter.

"That's odd. The bullet was going up, but Tom Duncan was either above him, standing up, shooting down, or at least level with him. How did that happen?" I asked.

"Ricochet like off the hill or a rock?"

"Nope. Not possible—the hump in the field obscured him from the middle of his back up and he was twenty or thirty feet beyond the hump. We saw that when we were there. If the bullet ricocheted up on any angle for that distance, it would have gone over his head."

"So, what are you saying, Tobias?"

"I'm saying that, to me, as painful and traumatic as it was for Tom Duncan, his statement doesn't match the facts. Except for the dragging out of the woods part, which he might have said just because he was so freaked out, I'm not sure there is anything in his statement that is actually untrue."

"That doesn't make any sense. It can't be wrong and right at the same time."

"Yeah, it can. What did the police chief say? Does his statement line up?" I asked.

"It looks like he typed this statement the day of the incident. It is labeled 'Investigation/Arrest Report.'

I was abruptly awakened to a disturbance in my bedroom at about 6:30 in the morning by Tom Duncan, who I knew. The young boy was in my bedroom. He was in a very excited state of mind, close to a hysterical situation. I asked him what was wrong and through his sobbing he said, "I think I killed a man." I got him to the kitchen where I questioned him further and asked him where he had been. He told me he had been over at the Chesterfield place. He said he thought it was a deer but when he got over to it, he realized it was a man. He said he tried CPR, but it didn't do any good. He told me he tried to carry the man out but couldn't. I asked him if he knew who it was and he said, "It was John Hamilton."

My wife had reached the kitchen and I asked her to get Wilson Ambulance on the line. I told them they were needed at the Chesterfield home out by the Old Range Road and to go Code 3. Then I called Tom Duncan's father, Corporal Duncan, told him what had happened and asked him to get over there right away and I would meet him there with his son. I then called the State Police Troop F and told them what had happened asked them to send a Fish & Game officer and a Trooper.

When I got to the scene, I saw the form of a man lying on the ground at the edge of the field near the tree line. I was unable to find a pulse in either the wrist or the neck. Within minutes, Cpl. Duncan arrived, and we placed his son in his car. Shortly thereafter, Wilson Ambulance arrived. Not having been able to locate a pulse, I asked my headquarters to call the medical referee. Fish & Game Officer Robert Lachance arrived, and I advised him as to who the parties were and, since I was a friend of both parties, I wanted him to handle the investigation.

Other officers arrived at the scene: a state trooper, a detective corporal, a sergeant and a deputy sheriff. I asked the sergeant to assist Robert Lachance in the investigation. Photographs were taken by the deputy sheriff. Officer Lachance called Dr. Inder for him to act as medical referee. At approximately 8:30 I went to my home with the doctor and Sergeant Harris to locate Jim Lacey to obtain his assistance in breaking the news to Mr. Hamilton's wife.

Upon advising him of the situation, we went to the Hamilton's home. Mrs. Hamilton became very emotional and hysterical. It took a considerable amount to time to calm her down. Jim Lacey and I remained at the house until a friend arrived to stay with her. Jim Lacey and I returned to my residence where he called the Concord office of the FBI to advise them of what had taken place. Two agents arrived at my house at about noon time.

"What's Code 3?" I asked Maggie.

"Sirens and lights. He said he called his headquarters. I thought he's the only cop in town. What headquarters? His wife?"

"And why," I asked, "did the three of them go back to the policeman's house to find Jim Lacey if they knew he had gone hunting on the other side of the mountain an hour ago? Why would they find him back at the chief's house? Doesn't he have his own home in town?"

"Maybe because he didn't know where Lacey was and, like he said, they were all going hunting at 9:00. He expected him to be there."

"Could be, but one thing is for sure. Lacey wasn't at the chief's house at 5:45 in the morning even though he had, for some unexplained reason, stayed overnight there. He was gone very early in the morning, way before sunrise. He would have to have had all his stuff with him: rifle, bullets, clothing, boots, maybe food and water—as if he expected to go hunting from that house, not his own."

"Why do you say, 'very early'?"

"Look at the map. We have to assume Hamilton was walking because there is no mention of his car. It's about a mile from his place to the field. That's a half-hour walk. Hamilton was dead at

6:10. The path, the only path to the Chesterfield house goes right in front of Chief Stone's house so Hamilton would have been there, at Stone's house expecting to meet up with his buddies, no later than a quarter to six. But Lacey either wasn't there or didn't come out. Also, If Hamilton thought they were going hunting at nine, like the other two, why was he there at six?"

"Let's look at the police reports. They might mention a car."

They did not mention a car. The Uniform Hunter Casualty Report, filled out by F&G Officer Lachance, said when and where the incident occurred, how the bullet traveled (from right shoulder to left side of neck), who the doctor was, who the shooter and victim were, that they both were licensed, that the shooter had been hunting deer with a rifle, that he mistook the victim for game, that the victim was in an open field in poor visibility and that he was obscured from the shoulders down.

A State Police Supplementary Report outlined who was there, that a spent 30-06 casing was found at the well house and that it was 241 feet from where the victim was shot. It also said the body was taken to the Littleton hospital for a post-mortem, but apparently all they did was undress him and look at the wound. Then somebody decided the body had to be transported to Mary Hitchcock Hospital in Hanover, an hour and a half away. *En route*, the ambulance stopped at the county attorney's office to discuss the case with him.

"The body, on the way to an autopsy, like where they determine the exact time of death, was hanging around in an ambulance in a parking lot, getting stiff, while they all just chatted it up with the DA. What's that about?"

"Why couldn't they do the autopsy at the local hospital? Is it too small?

"No, it's a big regional hospital, but you're right, Maggie. Why would all five officers go all the way from Pequot Falls to Hanover to witness an autopsy of a guy who they all know got shot in a hunting accident? And why did they have to discuss the case with the county attorney? What case? A hunting accident? What does a DA have to do with a hunting accident? That's all Fish & Game."

"That does seem weird," Maggie said, "it must have been a convoy. I've never seen a policeman ride in the back seat of a cruiser. As a matter of fact, they don't. There would have been a Fish & Game cruiser, a State Police cruiser and somebody riding shotgun in the ambulance. Some big deal since they all already knew how he died and they all had seen the wound at the local hospital when they undressed the guy."

"So, Maggie what's the biggest problem here?"

I got up and tapped my finger on the next document, a nine-page New Hampshire State Police Investigation Report.

"Fish & Game was in charge of this investigation and they closed it with their findings. The biggest problem is that Chief Stone gave the investigation to the Fish & Game people, as if it was a slam dunk that it was a hunting accident and their officer, after asking the boy what happened, sent him away with his father, the state trooper. Therefore, they investigated it as a hunting accident with a known conclusion. Ergo, no investigation. The kid saw brown, saw white, saw brown and shot. Tom Duncan was whisked away by his father before the police even got there. They didn't interview him, not there, not ever. He just gave his statement the next day after they had wrapped it all up. Ergo, no investigation. Then, the State Police do get involved and they take over. Fish & Game goes back to doing what they do—like estimating moose populations. Why?"

"Because John Hamilton was a nationally known FBI agent? An important guy?"

"Or, Maggie, one of the State Police thought it might not be as simple as a hunting accident and they wanted to control the information or somebody from Concord or Washington told them to get their arms around it and keep it tight and out of the public eye. Remember, they wouldn't give us any of this. A big, fat no."

"Why do you think there might be something funny here? Wasn't Tom Duncan telling the truth?"

"Oh, I think he was. He said he saw what he thought was a deer, aimed and shot then walked the field, saw white again when he was half-way there. That's important because he wasn't, at half-way, close enough to see Hamilton—he had to walk another 25 yards over the hump before he saw a man lying there, maybe dead, maybe not. That doesn't mean he shot the man—it means he thought he did."

"So, when he saw white again from the middle of the field, it couldn't have been Mr. Hamilton. It had to be something else."

"Right, and look at this." She handed me the Processed Property Report. They both had Remington 742 rifles, Duncan's with a four-power scope. On the ground near the rifles was Duncan's red cap and a pair of red cloth gloves. The gloves were listed as 'believed to be property of Hamilton'. Hamilton was wearing blue corduroy trousers, blue socks, white undershorts, leather boots, a white tee-shirt, a green/black shirt and a red and black jacket. The green/black shirt was buttoned at the collar. Didn't *The New York Times* quote the Fish & Game guy as saying, 'Nothing that I saw would have shown white.' Didn't he say that?"

"Yes, and that makes sense. John Hamilton's Rule #7—*Don't Wear Any Visible White.*"

She pointed to the photograph of the shirt with the bullet holes in it. It was red and white checkered, not red and black. "Different jacket. State Police, logging in evidence at a crime scene, do not get the color of a jacket wrong. I can't imagine that. Different jacket—somebody shot a hole through it. No wonder they had to take some time driving to Hanover. Someone told them, probably Fish & Game, that Tom Duncan had repeatedly said that he saw white. And the red gloves? They weren't Tom Duncan's, he said they weren't his. The police listed them as Hamilton's, but they were definitely not John Hamilton's. You can't get shot through the back and neck and take your gloves off before you face-plant on the ground. Nobody said they took his gloves off him. Why would they? If they were on his body, they would've been in his back pocket. If they were in his hand, how did he hold his rifle? In one hand? Nope. Where did the gloves come from?"

"What do you think happened, Tobias?"

"Tom Duncan saw a deer, shot at it and missed. John Hamilton was already mortally wounded or dead when Duncan pulled the trigger. Maybe even before Duncan showed up to hunt. Somebody else shot him in the back and some state trooper was beginning to figure that out. The bullet was going up, not down." I remembered what he said on the note in the toaster:

If you hear of my accidental death, don't believe it. It will have been murder.

12

THERE IT WAS, STARING RIGHT OUT AT ME. State Police Report, page 3: *'Both rifles were found to be in off safe position. The victim's rifle had a round in the chamber.'* Mr. Hamilton told me—must have been a dozen times—Rule #6, do not walk with a loaded rifle, do not load a round in the chamber until you know the quarry is there, do not take the rifle off safety until it is in your sight and you intend to shoot. And there it was—he saw his quarry and intended to shoot. At what? A deer? The same deer that Tom Duncan saw? A man? A what? He saw something, that's for sure. He would never have loaded the chamber and taken the gun off safety unless there was something right there within his vision that needed to be shot. Had there been a man in the woods in front of him, a man he knew was sent to murder him? And was that man then behind him, crouched down below the hump in the field, with a pistol and a silencer? Did Hamilton hear him and click off the safety? A man who shot him in the back before Tom Duncan even showed up?

"Tobias, I don't like the long straw. I can't be the good guy anymore. Things are not right here."

"I agree. Look at these." One was a letter from Tom Duncan's father to the Commander of the State Police. The father resigned from the department and he was demanding the rifle back. It had been given to little Tom by his grandfather as a present on his twelfth birthday and the case was now closed. There was no law preventing them from returning the rifle. The charge had been a misdemeanor, not a felony. A second letter was from the County Attorney, copied to the Commander, denying the request with no rationale for the decision. Mr. Duncan had filed suit in local court and then mysteriously withdrew the suit the next day. Another was a similar suit filed by Mrs. Hamilton, alleging a wrongful death. It didn't specify how the death was wrongful, but it too had been withdrawn the following day.

She said, "Somebody with an awfully big stick got to these poor people almost instantly and, for some reason, caused them both to drop their lawsuits and shut up."

Darkness came early. Sometime in the afternoon it faded from day to grey and then, long before dinnertime, it darkened, quickly blackened and the air turned cold. A few inches of snow had fallen. The stars were pinpoint, little dots of twinkling bright, white lights. There were no shadows—a dark clothed man walking boldly down a path could not be seen, but he could be heard. Nothing he could do would mask the sound. The snow was so dry it crunched under every footstep. Maggie and I turned all the lights out, so we could sip our brandy on the porch in the pitch dark and watch the stars shimmer. She nestled up tight to me and put her head on my shoulder. We both heard the crunch in the snow.

Maggie's head snapped up and she whispered, "Someone's out there."

Then more crunches coming closer.

"Hello, hello. Who's out there?" I yelled.

A bright light, brighter than a flashlight, bright as a headlight, turned on directly in our faces. Maggie screamed, and I froze. She dropped to the floor, dragging me down with her. We crawled to a spot behind the solid porch railing. A pistol shot ripped into the wood wall behind us. The light went out and the crunches, rapid now, were the sound of a person running away.

We huddled behind the railing, breathing deep and slow, until there were no sounds save the faint deep "hoo-hoo-ho hooo" of an owl off in the forest. Maggie was twisting locks of her hair on her finger and chewing on it.

"Well, Maggie, they didn't want to kill us or they would have. They're sending us a message and they ripped a hole in my mother's house. Fuckers. I think we should turn the porch lights on and you should take pictures of those documents with your smartphone and e-mail them to me at the *Globe*. Let's leave the paper copies here. Let them steal them and think they got it all. We'll have the photo'd ones when we get back. Then let's get out of here."

"I don't like the thought of driving out of here in the dark. A lot of things could happen and none of them are good."

"Then let's go up to the hotel and stay there for the night. It's public and the doors would get locked at night. It's way safer and there's a bar there."

The Presidential Inn is a place where wealthy tourists stay when they come to whitewater raft in the spring, hike and camp in the summer, look at the foliage in the fall or ski the mountains in the winter. The bar is appointed to appeal to the tastes of the well-heeled. They can find rustic charm and cheap draft beer at any of a dozen places scattered about in the near-by towns, but here the seats are upholstered leather set around granite topped coffee tables and the bar is an immaculate, varnished slab of oak cut from these woods a hundred years ago with copper edging and polished brass foot rails. The bartender wears a bowtie and the beers, all imported, cost eight bucks apiece.

Maggie had told the matronly woman at the check-in desk that she was, and she lowered her voice, having a bit of a problem with a jealous boyfriend and did she have a room that was quite secure? The woman pointed up the staircase to a door at the top of the stairs and said, in a Miss Marple innocent but all-knowing kind of way, that from her desk she could see everyone who went near that door. At ten o'clock, after the bar closes, the front doors are locked and only those with a room key can get inside. Then she looked at me as though I had been apprehended for statutory rape.

The great lawyer was still at the Inn, sitting alone at a table, reading legal papers of some sort, sipping a drink that had a cherry floating in it. I asked if we could join him for a moment. His response was southern gentleman at its best.

"Why I would be truly honored with your presence." He looked back to the bar and snapped his fingers. "Whatever you would wish to drink shall be put on my tab. And no argument about it. If I recall properly, you are Tobias, the reporter, and just who might this delectable damsel be?"

Maggie actually curtsied, as though he was British nobility and said, "My name is Maggie James, Mr. Conklin. It is truly my pleasure to make your acquaintance." Where did she get that shit? Certainly not her father. She ordered a whiskey sour, just like, I now figured out, the great one was sipping. A slow nod of his head seemed to mean it pleased him that she could tell a drink by looking at it. Very shortly, I was cut out of the conversation and Maggie described to him how we had gotten the documents and all the findings we had reached from reviewing them.

He then turned to me. "When we first talked on the porch, I asked you to contact me if you found anything that might merit a poor lawyer's attention. My interest was piqued. Since then, I have checked with a few sources in Washington. The information that Mr. Hamilton was going to divulge to the Senate Select Committee was his alone. No one else knew what it was, at least no one in the FBI. It did not come from within this country. That means your problem is not the FBI, it is the CIA. That is far more dangerous to you. They do not need warrants to kill people. My sources revealed that they thought the CIA didn't know what Mr. Hamilton's files actually contained, but they did know what it pertained to. It pertained to the president of the United States and whether his election was legitimate and, equally problematic, whether he is even fit to hold office. That is all I know, and I suspect that is all *they* know but it seems to be enough to have gotten Mr. Hamilton killed. By the way, there were two other people who were going to testify that day. Strangely, they were both healthy young women and even more strangely, one died of a massive heart attack and the other fell off a five-hundred-foot-tall cliff in Big Sur the same day Mr. Hamilton passed away. So, on judicial reflection, I must retract my offer of assistance. I would prefer," he said as he chewed his cherry, "not to eat Agent Orange. I don't particularly want my face to fall off and land in my drink." He snapped his fingers again for the bartender and ordered another round.

"Tobias," said Maggie suddenly, "see that guy who just sat at the bar? That's Jim Lacey, it's got to be him. Short blonde hair, six-four, walks with a slight limp. That's him, just like Daddy described him." She fished in her purse and brought out her smartphone, clicked it on to record and put it in my shirt pocket. "Put your jacket on and go ask him where he was hunting."

The lawyer pushed his chair back, snapped his suspenders, pushed his whiskey sour in front of Maggie and said, "I believe I will take my leave now. You both seem to be carelessly brave." He took Maggie's hand and kissed it. "I wish I was young and foolish again. Take care, both of you." With that, he waddled out the back door onto the deck and took a sharp left, quickly out of sight.

"Mr. Lacey, I was a friend of John Hamilton. I understand you were also his friend. I am now a reporter for the *Boston Globe* and I'm trying to find out exactly what happened and how it happened. Do you mind if I ask you a few questions?"

He turned to me slowly. His eyes were not blue as Maggie's dad had said, they were darker than blue, more like the blued steel of a gun barrel and his jaw wasn't square as Johnny James had said, it was massive, like his jawbone was the largest bone in his body. He put his face a few inches from mine and I squirmed back as far as my seat would go without tipping over.

"I refuse to get involved." That is all he said. He pushed his stool back, stood all six-four tall, stared down at me, squared his shoulders, tossed a ten spot on the bar and left by the front door.

"Refuse to get involved? Involved in what? It's over. A hunting accident. A misdemeanor, nothing more. Done, over, water under the bridge. Don't you think he could have said, 'Yes, he was my friend, I'm deeply sorry about his death. I wish I had been there with him. It might never have happened.' But he didn't say anything like that, he said, 'I refuse to get involved!' What does that mean?"

I didn't want to listen to the tape again. I couldn't understand it and hearing it only brought back the instant fear I felt when he pushed his face into mine. I wanted to snuggle up in the king-sized bed and leave it all behind. The great one, Mr. Conklin had left it all behind and I now wanted to do the same. The trauma of it all was starting to eat away at my mind. I didn't trust myself anymore. It was like I was back on Black Bear Hill with a wet tuna fish sandwich leaking all over my pants, crying for Mr. Hamilton. Lacey's growl had been the growl of an angry bear. I put my fingers on Maggie's lips and pushed her head gently into the voluminous, tasseled pillow. The inn may have been five-star, but the king-sized bed still squeaked as we wrapped the comforters around our bodies and intertwined as tight as two vines in a thicket.

All the documents were gone. There was a note on blank paper in pencil—it look like it had been written by a right-handed person using their left hand. *'LEAVE US ALONE'.*

"Well." Maggie said, "it's either a local person or somebody who wants us to think the locals want us gone."

"It is most definitely not a local person. They would have put the note on the front door and they would not have stolen the papers. My guess is it was whoever shot at us. It's good you photographed all of them and sent them to Jasmine. I think we should leave now, close up the house and get back to Boston so I can write my story without getting shot."

We pulled into the country store to buy some trail mix and iced tea for the ride home and there, across the road at the edge of a field, was Tom Duncan. He was standing, hands in his pockets looking out at the mountains. As I began to cross the road, he saw me, stared at me, then turned and walked away, into the woods.

"That poor boy." Maggie said. Deer season was open for another week, but he wasn't allowed to get a license to hunt for ten years as part of his fine. He was dressed in full hunting camouflage with an orange cap and no gun. All dressed up and nowhere to go. Wandering the woods with no direction home. "That poor, poor boy. He thinks he shot a man, a man he knew and liked. He thinks he killed him. I wish we could tell him it might not have been like that at all—that something else might have happened."

"We'd never find him out there, or anywhere. I doubt he wants to talk anybody."

A bell, tied to a string, tinkled when we opened the door. Beanie was behind the counter, just like the last time I saw him, his crutches leaned against the tobacco shelf behind him, left pant leg pinned up at the knee.

"Hello Beanie, I'm Tobias Starkey. Years ago, you and your brother drove me to the Youth Hunt party out at Jenson Pond. Do you remember?" No answer. No reaction. "This is my friend Maggie James. She's from Boston. Maggie, this is Beanie Weeks."

He was looking at Maggie, slowly up and down her body. His eyes fixed on her breasts. Maggie zipped up her jacket.

"Beanie, whatever happened to Mary Sue Lynxe?"

"She did real good in school and went off to some fancy-assed college. But she was all knocked up when she got there, and people say she had to drop out after a few months. A friend of hers said she moved up to Canada and got shot by her boyfriend, but I don't believe it. Her friend's dumber than a sack of rocks. A real whack-job. I don't know what Mary Sue saw in her. She don't know nothin'. Girls like Mary Sue don't get shot, they do the shootin'."

"What college, Beanie? Where'd she go to college?"

"I dunno. Like I said, it was one of those hotsy-totsy schools down-state."

"Was it Dartmouth? Is that the school?"

"Yeah, that's it. That's what her friend said. That Mary Sue, she was the best piece of ass in this whole county. Bar none. Believe you me, I know." His eyes went back to the bulges in Maggie's zipped-up jacket.

Maggie held out two bags of trail mix, put a five-dollar bill on the counter and dragged me out by my sleeve. "Jesus, Tobias, that guy's creepy. This whole place is giving me the major creeps."

As we were walking to the door, Beanie said, "Funny you should ask about that. That friend of yours who got shot, the old guy who helped me with my deer that year, he came in a while back and asked the same damn questions about her. World's a funny place, ain't it?"

On the way back to Boston, cruising down the Interstate past the hamlets spread out in the foothill valleys, Maggie asked me to tell her the story of Beanie Weeks. What was that all about? What happened to his leg? And who was this Mary Sue Lynxe girl? Did you know her? I mean, like, biblically?

13

BEANIE WEEKS HAD A BONER FOR MARY SUE. That's what I found out on my way to the first big party I was ever invited to. I was fifteen. I had just entered the ninth grade and had bagged my first deer that day out on Black Bear Hill. I was with Mr. Hamilton at the dead deer registration center which was a room on the back of the country store in town. You fill out all the paperwork and leave the deer there. The old man who owns the store cuts it up, you pay him some money and, a few days later, you pick up venison wrapped in brown paper and put it in your freezer.

Another kid about my age was also registering his deer and we got to talking. He said there was going to be a keg party that night in the woods behind Jenson Pond and any high school student who had gotten a deer that year was automatically invited, even if they didn't live in Pequot Falls. It was a high school tradition in Pequot Falls that happened every year on the last day of Youth Hunt. He said the cops knew about it but never bothered anybody because of the deer thing. The door to manhood. There were a lot of girls that came. Everybody had to kick in five bucks for the beer.

I told him I didn't have any way of getting there; the transmission in our car was busted. It wasn't really a lie. My mother had complained about how hard it was to put the car in reverse, but there was no way I was going to get dropped off out there by my mother.

Even if I could convince her to do it, which was not likely, that is not how you arrive at your first keg party. He said he'd pick me up at seven and asked where I lived.

I was right. My mother didn't like the idea at all. It's illegal and dangerous. Kids can get hurt. Children should not start drinking alcohol at that young an age, etc., etc., etc. But I had waited until quarter of seven to tell her about it, figuring that she would likely go on for fifteen minutes or so about why it was such a bad idea and by then Beanie would be out front waiting for me. What would she do then? Make me go out there and tell him my mother wouldn't let me go? No, she wouldn't. She'd tell me to be responsible, be careful and come home early and I'd assure her that I certainly would do all of that.

A horn beeped and there was the old truck that had been at the registration place. I gave her a hug, grabbed my hunting jacket and dashed out.

Some long piece of farm-type equipment was attached to the rear bumper. In the back of the truck there were three shiny barrels that I assumed were kegs of beer. An older kid was behind the wheel. He was Buckie, Beanie's brother. Behind the seat, across the rear window, hanging in a metal rack, was a hunting rifle. I handed Beanie my five-dollar bill.

"I'm Tobias. Thanks for picking me up. Nice truck."

"Yeah," Buckie said, "my dad gave it to me when I got my license, but I've been driving it around since I was ten. It's beat up, but it runs good."

"What's that machine you're towing behind the truck?"

"Never seen one of those bad boys? Guess you're not from up here. That's a wood splitter. Where we're going to there's a big pile of stumps too big to burn, so we're going to spilt 'em up for a bonfire."

"Do your parents know about this keg party?" I asked.

"My dad thinks we're going to the high school to play basketball."

"My mom really didn't like the idea of all us kids drinking in the woods."

"Nobody's mom thinks it's a good idea," Beanie said. "If they did, they'd be a shitty mom. Like, if they drive somebody out there and something bad happens, Chief Stone would probably arrest *her* just for being a shitty mom. Sure hope Mary Sue is here. She is so hot."

"Boy oh boy," Buckie said, "you sure got a boner for that girl. You ain't getting anywhere with her. She's seventeen and you're a punk kid in the ninth grade. Forget it."

Buckie drove down a narrow dirt path around the edge of the pond, then backed the wood splitter up near a pile of short fat logs. The thing was a frame with wheels and a long tongue to hook to the back bumper, a big motor, a piston with a sharpened wedge and a solid block of steel at the end.

There were already twenty or so kids there. They all gathered around giving Beanie their five bucks and helping drag the beer kegs out of the back and setting them up under an oak tree. A fire was started inside a circle of rocks.

I got a good look at Mary Sue Lynxe. She was standing by the fire, eyes closed, a smile on her fat red lips, arms spread out wide like she was inviting the whole world to come in close for a hug. She was dynamite. The flames gave a flickering glow to her wavy red hair and her dress, a simple thing cinched tight around her waist by a wide black belt, made her body explode. With the light of the fire behind,

I could see right through it. Her underclothes were pink. Buckie was dead-on right—she wasn't giving up any of that for a gap-toothed fifteen-year-old. Why would she?

But Beanie was oblivious. He didn't realize how foolish he looked elbowing other guys aside, drinking beer after beer and telling her all about how he shot the deer right through the eyeball, gutted it all by himself and dragged it a mile through the woods. This went on for a long time before she backed away and moved a big guy right in front of her.

An hour into the party the woods were full of kids. Beanie was drunk, staggering around, still trying to get close to Mary Sue.

The first beer I drank was the first beer I had ever drunk, and it was bitter. I didn't like it. I was planning my exit. I needed to get home. I couldn't find Buckie anywhere and no one knew for sure where he had gone. One guy said he was 'out there,' gesturing to the forest beyond, with a girl named Ginger. I started moving from group to group to see if I could catch wind of anybody driving back near town. I didn't know anybody, and nobody knew me.

One group was talking about who was the best young hunter in Grafton County and they all agreed it was a guy sitting alone at the base of a tree. He was wearing a cowboy hat pulled down low, so I couldn't see his eyes. His name was Tom Duncan and he had been hunting since he was eight and had bagged a deer every year. Never bragged about it. His dad was a state trooper and Tom was known as a very careful hunter and an expert marksman. Didn't shoot unless he had a clean shot. Probably could drop one from five hundred yards.

The wood splitter was running but nobody was working it. I heard Beanie yell out, "Hey Mary Sue, watch this!" and I saw Beanie run to jump over the wood splitter. I saw Beanie not make it over the splitter. I saw him trip and fall over backwards and I saw Beanie with his leg over the machine and the sleeve of his arm caught in the lever and I saw the steel wedge move. I saw Beanie thrash and hump his body up and I saw the wedge push his leg toward the steel block and I heard him scream and I couldn't move. I couldn't move, I couldn't make a noise and then everyone heard Beanie scream and scream as the splitter slowly, slowly severed his leg completely off above the knee.

Tom Duncan was the first to move. He was there in a second, slamming the lever down to move it back, hitting the kill switch, holding Beanie's head in the crook of his arm, yelling at me to give him my knife. He yelled at anyone to call 911, to call his dad, Trooper Duncan. Get them out here! Get him a blanket. He cut the pant leg off, cut it in half and told me to hold Beanie's head off the hot motor and he pulled the pant leg back and tied a tourniquet with a knot in it around the thigh, took a stick and twisted the cloth tight, tighter, and tighter until the blood stopped gushing out of the stump. Beanie was unconscious. The hot muffler was burning a hole through the arm of my new hunting jacket. I kept it there, holding Beanie's head, waiting for Tom Duncan to tell me what to do next. I still have an ugly scar on the back of my right arm.

It made the second page of the state-wide newspaper. There was a picture of Chief Stone under the banner—PEQUOT FALLS POLICE CHIEF ORDERS END TO YOUTH HUNT PARTIES. The caption below his picture was a quote. "*I am very disappointed in the parents of our children for letting this terrible kind of thing happen. Parents need to be more involved with their children.*"

Did he have any idea how stupid that statement was? The article went on and on about how the government shouldn't be the babysitter, taxpayers shouldn't have to pay for programs to do the work of the parents, but it never stated the obvious. He was the cop. Controlling that party was his job. He knew about it year after year and let it go on. He might just as well have chopped off Beanie Weeks' leg himself, but instead, he was considering charges against George and Emily Weeks.

I learned a huge amount in that one evening out in the woods—about girls and boys, about alcohol, about courage. The next day, reading that newspaper with gauze bandages wrapped around my arm, I learned about the meanness, the self-preservation instincts of public officials and about the failings of a press that supports one political view or another. All of it set me on my path to becoming a journalist.

Beanie Weeks lived. I saw him every once in a while, sitting on that stool behind the counter in the country store with his crutches leaned against the tobacco shelf behind him, left pant leg pinned up at the knee. He never seemed to recognize me.

Mary Sue Lynxe got pregnant and went off to live with her grandmother someplace in Canada. Years later, ten years later to be exact, I heard a lot about Tom Duncan. About how he mistook John Hamilton for a deer and shot him, but, except for that night in the woods when Mary Sue spread her arms and let the firelight flow through her dress, that night that Beanie's leg got chopped off, I've never spoken a word to him.

14

JASMINE HAD THE DOCUMENTS all printed out, paper clipped in packets, arranged in chronological order. She met me at a restaurant a few blocks from the *Globe*'s office.

"I could get in trouble for this. Maybe even fired. Sam Borstien keeps grumbling about you. Talking about hiring somebody 'reliable' to take your place."

"Why would you get in trouble?"

"You know the rule. Information that comes onto a secretary's desk is available to anyone. It's not protected source information. He keeps asking if I have seen anything from you. I lied and said no. Now that you have all this, can you just write your story and go on with life?"

"No, I'm not done yet. There's something I need to find, and I don't have any idea where it is. No idea even where to look. I followed him to the end of his path where he died in the field and found nothing."

"What's that, Tobias? What do you need to find?"

"Some papers."

"Not that I'm supposed to know anything, but wouldn't the FBI have all of them? I mean, he did work for them."

"They don't have them, and they really want them. I think that's why he died."

"By the way, people's paths don't end where they die, they get buried you know, usually somewhere else. What's in these papers that they want so much?"

"I can't tell you that. I've already told you too much. I'm going to have a turkey club sandwich and an iced tea. What about you? It's on me. I'm paying."

"I can keep a secret, you know."

"No, Jasmine, you may want to, but I don't think you could. Not if Borstien wants to know and not if you really don't want to get fired. The FBI can get to Borstien either backchannel or through a court. And Borstien can get to you. It's better you know nothing."

"Then fine, I'll have some cucumber slices, carrots and a glass of water. No ice."

She was miffed. I called the waiter over and placed our order. There were two men sitting a few tables over who kept glancing our way. They wore suits. It wasn't unusual for people to be dressed up here because it was so close to City Hall, but, on a lunch break, people tended to talk and joke or be earnest as they cut some deal. These guys weren't talking to each other. They were looking at me. They were close cropped square-jawed forty-year-olds wearing cheap suits that hung all wrong. Forty-year-olds who work in City Hall don't wear cheap suits. They get paid good money to look sharp when they're dealing with the public, the voters. I was getting paranoid. Don't run, don't panic. Talk to Jasmine like we're co-workers. Friends, but not really good friends. Co-workers out for lunch. Talk about the office. Talk about cucumbers.

That afternoon, I called Maggie at work. "Do you think your Dad or his buddies in the bar could spot an FBI guy?"

"A mile away, why?"

"I think I'm being followed. I think they were in the restaurant where I went for lunch with Jasmine and I think they're sitting in a car outside my apartment. Can you meet me at your Dad's bar after work?"

"See you there at 5:30."

I parked in the handicap spot. I had a plan and I was going to need to get out fast. I was pretty sure any cop who thought about giving the car a ticket would go in and check with Johnny James first.

The first part of the plan was just to get somewhere else without being followed. The second part was to figure out what Jim Lacey meant when he said, 'I refuse to get involved'. I might get a handle on that in Cambridge, across the Charles River. The third part came from something Jasmine had said at the restaurant. She said people's paths don't end where they die, they end where they get buried. That's the 'final resting place.' Hudson, Massachusetts.

I kissed Maggie. Not anything hot and steamy, just enough so that Johnny James would know we were still together, still tight. I told him that I was in the handicap spot and he allowed as how he didn't give a shit. As Maggie was telling him all about our trip north, the two guys in their cheap suits came in, made their way to the end of the bar and waited to get served.

"Daddy, are those guys FBI?"

"I'd say that's pretty likely. Why?"

"Because Tobias thinks he's being followed."

"You want me to make sure?"

"Yes."

He went down the bar and asked them what they wanted to drink. He served them two cups of coffee and then went to the table of county prosecutors and had a word with them. Then he stopped

119

at a table of three beefy cops. They were sitting with a tall, heavily made-up blonde woman. He served some more drinks and came back to us.

"Nobody knows them but it's 100% certain they're feds. Why, young man, would they be following you?"

"I haven't got all the documents yet and I think they want to see where I go. I think they're looking for the same thing I am."

"And what's that?"

"Mr. James, I wish I could tell you, but I can't. Not yet. I need to lose those feds. Do you see any way they could be, I don't know, maybe detained or diverted or something so I can get out of here without them seeing me? I think I need about five minutes. I would be really thankful if that could happen."

He looked up and down the bar, out into the room with tables.

"This could be fun. Maggie, I want you to go home now. I mean right now. They know you're with him," he said, dipping his head toward me, "and I'm sure they know you're my daughter. They may want to get some information out of you. Scoot."

I gave her my cell phone. "They can track this thing. I have my credit card, lots of cash, and just in case I need it, my passport." She took the phone and scooted.

Johnny James served a customer at the bar, a large fellow with a bald head, talked to him a bit, then mixed a drink and carried it over to the table with the three cops and the blonde woman. He gave her the drink and leaned closer, talking in her ear, then came back behind the bar and began chatting it up with some local guys. Then he made a phone call.

The feds had their eye on me. I could feel it. After about five minutes, the woman got up and seemed to stagger to the bar and wrapped her arms around the stout, bald man nursing his beer. I realized she wasn't a blonde woman, she was a drag queen. He shrugged her off and she careened, goofy-footed and lopsided right in between the two FBI guys, arms around both of them, skirt up, bosoms everywhere.

Then she screamed, "Get your hands out of my panties, you creep!" The three cops who had been sitting with the drag queen were on their feet in a second and bulled their way into the melee. I dashed for the door, into my car and down the street. In my rearview, I saw a police car, lights on, pull into the spot I'd left and two cops dash into the Old South Ender. Reinforcements to join in the fun. I had time.

Up to State Street onto Cambridge Street, across the Longfellow Bridge, past MIT, down Broadway past Harvard Square, all the way out Mt. Auburn and back down Highway 20 until I came to a Super 8 motel. Perfect. Nobody pulling in behind me, no peering eyes in the lobby. I had ditched them, thanks to Johnny James and Boston's finest.

I spent the early twilight hours walking the greenbelt trails along the Charles. The river was frozen at the banks. There was a wide stream of rippling water in the middle, the air was cold, but the paths were free of snow. No one was there but me. I wandered for miles, down to Watertown Square then back along the river's edge over the Braille Trail and down to the Watertown Yacht Club and Marina.

As I walked back to the motel, alone and getting cold, I realized I had no idea what I was doing. Not that I didn't have a plan, I did, but it wasn't a plan devised by someone who had done this before. I remembered what Mike Tyson had said, *Everyone's got a plan 'til they get punched in the mouth.* That was the problem. That could happen.

I was swinging in the ring and couldn't see the other guy—just flailing away at a ghost.

The motel seemed to be hosting a convention of some sort. The bar was full of middle-aged men in polo shirts talking earnestly about things that made no sense to me. For a while, I thought they dealt in recycled animal parts for dog food. They were discussing heels and tongues and throats and then I thought no, that's disgusting and there wouldn't be a whole pile of golf course looking guys who spent their lives hacking up dead animals. It must be high heels; throat chokers and tongue studs because they also were talking waists and breasts. They must all run strip clubs. At a table behind me someone mentioned vamps and welts. I figured they had a dominatrix room in the basement of their club. But it still made no sense. They didn't look like strip club owners. They all looked normal. I finally gave up and asked the bartender. They worked for Johnston & Murphy. They were shoe salesmen. I concluded that I stunk at figuring out what someone means by what they say. Tomorrow, I would learn all about that topic. Hopefully.

From my room, I called the main switchboard for Harvard University and got put through to the office of Dr. Alice Turnbell, professor of linguistics. It was after dinner. I didn't expect her to be in her office. She was.

"Dr. Turnbell, this is Tobias Starkey, we met at Lake Winnipesaukee at the Gemma Institute. Do you remember me?"

"Yes, yes Tobias, I do. Of course I do. How are you?"

"Fine. I'm fine, thank you, but I really need your help. I'm in a bit of jam and it is a somewhat dangerous situation. If you could help me understand a sentence, just a five-word sentence that was said to me by an FBI agent, I would really appreciate it."

"And... what is that sentence?"

"Out of context, it wouldn't mean anything and, that context is complicated. Is there any possibility I could come by your office tomorrow? I don't mean to sound pushy but I do have a pretty big problem. Is there any chance you'll be in tomorrow?

"Yes, I'd love to see you. Come by anytime between nine and noon. Boylston Hall, room 223."

"Thank you so much, Doctor. God willing, I'll be there."

Harvard Square on a warm, clear winter's day. The chess boards were out, the buskers sang and danced on every corner. Some souls were in tee shirts and shorts. Snow and slush were melting from the curbs and running down the storm drains. The outside café tables were full — people sipping lattes and talking art, literature, science, politics.

I was happy to be there, comfortable, sitting on a bench watching the day unfold. Harvard Square is one of those rare places in the country where an FBI agent would stand out like a zebra on a horse ranch.

At eleven thirty, I walked through gates to Harvard Yard and into Boylston Hall, read the faculty directory in the lobby and went up a flight of stairs to room 223. The sign on the door said, *Alice Turnbell*. No *Prof., Dr.*, or *PhD.*, like all the other names on all the other doors, even though I knew she was all of those. I knocked, and someone said, "Come in, come in."

The office was unlike any faculty office I had seen. It was spare and clean, not a single book on a shelf, one tidy stack of papers on the polished desk. A few paintings hung on the wall. They were African art and the window curtains, carpet and sofa upholstery had colors that matched the sand, ivory, blood red and jet black of the artwork. Dr. Turnbell had shoulder length wavy grey hair, wore gold hoop earrings and a pearl necklace on a black silk blouse. Her face was solid, like a fighter.

"I was pleased to get your call yesterday, Tobias. Did you enjoy your time at the Gemma Institute?"

"Very much so. I'm afraid I'm a bit too green to understand everything in a real-world context, but it seems I'm getting a pretty fast education now. The time I spent there really helps. It got me here to your office and I'm grateful you said you'd help."

"If I can, I will. What is it you're working on? A five-word sentence you need to understand? That doesn't seem difficult. Tell me all about it."

That simple request opened the floodgates and I couldn't hold back any longer. As she patiently waited for me to gather my thoughts, sitting at the other end of the sofa, I realized that this was a person nobody was going to get anything out of that she didn't want to give them, and she was shielded by one of the most prestigious universities in the world. I breathed deeply and went all-in. I talked. I talked for a long time, taking her all the way from the days I spent with John Hamilton more than ten years ago to the day I got hired at the *Globe* to the Sir John Motel and Pequot Falls and the bar at the Presidential Inn and back to yesterday in the Old North Ender.

"I'm assuming that a lot of what you just told me is protected by either journalistic privilege or your sheer will to stay alive. Why don't you treat me as a confidential source? Let's keep it that way. You were never here. Now, if I get it right, you are working on a story that maybe the whole world will read that asserts that Hamilton had private files that might seriously compromise the President of the United States. That he was murdered, possibly by his own government, a week before he was to testify about this to a secret select Senate Committee. Do I have it right?"

"Yes, except I won't publish the story until I have the files and I will publish those as part of my article."

"My Good Lord! Just when, Tobias, do you expect these people to murder you as well?"

"Not until I find the files. They don't know where they are either. Then, after I find them, before I can publish them, they will come after me. I will have to move fast and be invisible. I haven't figured any of that out yet because I don't know where to look."

"Okay." She went to her desk and wrote some things on a piece of paper. "This is the keypad code that will get you in to this building if you need it. This is the keypad number to my office. This room may be a safe haven for you. Please use it if you need it. This is my cell phone number. I wrote it four-digit, four-digit so it doesn't look like a phone number, and this the password to my computer. I will be gone the entire Christmas vacation but feel free to use to use my office if you need it. I'll tell the security folks you have my permission to be here. There is nothing personal or confidential on the computer. I always save that information to a remote device and delete from this one. Too many prying eyes." She gave it to me. I folded it and put it in my wallet. "Now, let's listen to that tape."

I turned it on to play. *Mr. Lacey, I was a friend of John Hamilton. I understand you were also his friend. I am now a reporter for the Boston Globe and I'm trying to find out exactly what happened and how it happened. Do you mind if I ask you a few questions?*

Then his answer. *I refuse to get involved.*

"He sounds like he comes from South Boston. Do you know if he does?"

"Yes, he was a policeman in Boston before the FBI hired him."

"He sounds angry. Angry with you because you're looking into it or angry with himself for not having been there or angry because he *does* know who shot him? He certainly couldn't be angry at John Hamilton for having gotten shot or angry with a young man out hunting who made a terrible mistake. If he was angry that he wasn't there to help, he would have said so. The local chief said he was hunting on the other side of the mountain?"

"Yes."

"Why wouldn't he have corroborated that story with something like, 'I wasn't there so, I'm sorry but there isn't anything I can add to what law enforcement has already determined.' Then everything is fine, all suspicion goes away. But he didn't — he said, 'I refuse'. To refuse to do something means you have to have been pressured or mandated to do that thing. In his case, to get involved."

"How would answering a question be 'getting involved'?"

"It wouldn't. If you refuse to get involved, it almost always means you know something or have firm beliefs about something, as in 'I refuse to get involved in my sister's love affairs.' Implied is that your involvement would come out badly for someone — her, you or the lovers. Can you play that tape again?"

I did.

She said, "He stressed the word 'involved.' I refuse to get INVOLVED. This man knows something that other people don't know, and he doesn't want to tell anyone what that is. That is clear to me. If he had stressed the word 'refuse,' it would indicate he has been asked before and doesn't want anything to do with it. But 'involved'? That means he believes it to be more complicated than a simple hunting accident. He knows how John Hamilton died and it likely isn't how others think it happened. Be careful of this man."

"That's what my girlfriend's father said. He knows him."

"Tobias, you can't refute an image with an explanation. The image does not go away — it was seen, it was there. No matter what you find, you will remember that man saying that to you and your gut reaction to that is probably the most important piece of information you will get." She stood. "Don't forget you have the keypad numbers and please, be careful."

"Thank you so much for the offer of your office. It might come to that. Thank you, Dr. Turnbell for all your help, you've been wonderful. I should go now."

"Alice," she said and put her hand on my shoulder. "Just Alice."

15

I WAS LOST. Lost like I had been when I was a child; fat, slow and unloved by anyone except my mother. It's possible she didn't love me either, just took care of me because I was hers and that's what she had to do. Maybe that happens with a lot with mothers. They wash your clothes, feed you, pack you off to school and then your father dies, and they marry someone else and go off with barely a decent good-bye. A kiss on the cheek and a quick hug but no tears. No trembling chin, no eyes welled up with tears to prove the love.

I had no idea why I was going to Hudson, Massachusetts. To stand alone in a cemetery and look at John Hamilton's gravestone? Did I think some divine inspiration would visit upon me? The stone would speak? One thing I was sure of, nobody, not a single living person, knew where I was or where I was going. I remembered an existential philosophy class at Dartmouth and realized that that infinite group of nobody included me.

In the early afternoon, I found the place where John Hamilton was buried. I parked at a convenience store on a hill above the graveyard and looked down over the expanse of mostly simple stone markers, some more ornate, carved memorials and a few monuments with statues and grand tall crosses. The entrance to Saint Michael Cemetery was framed in round brick pillars and an arched metal sign mostly covered in ivy. The cemetery was huge, probably twenty or thirty acres, bisected both ways by a dozen roads. Inside the vast lots defined by the roads were footpaths to graves on the interior of the lots. Thousands of graves.

A few cars were parked on the roads and small clusters of families planted fresh flowers. It was quiet and serene. For each of these families of three or four people, it seemed to be peaceful and private. I drove down the hill, through the entrance arch and parked somewhere near the middle of the graveyard. I walked up a road and then down a path looking at the stones to get a sense of the age of the cemetery or the ethnicity of the dearly departed. There was no pattern. There was no reason there should be. It was a Catholic graveyard, but there was no reason that everyone buried there was Catholic. Sons and daughters, nieces, nephews and grandchildren could all be buried in a family plot and come from different places and beliefs. It was not going to be possible to find one particular stone no matter how long I wandered the roads and paths. I needed to find someone who might know and ask them how to do that. Ask them where my friend was.

His funeral had been held in Saint Michael Parish — Paróquia de São Miguel, a Portuguese Catholic church not far from the center of town. The main doors on the front were closed. I walked around back, up a few steps to a landing, took hold of an iron knocker cast in the shape of a fish and rapped on the door. The door creaked open and I was welcomed in by an old woman in a black cloak, a cloth on her head and a fist-sized cross hanging around her neck. I sensed it was very bad luck to lie inside a holy chapel, so I stood outside on the steps and told her that my grandmother had gone to school in this town and she had been a very close friend of John Cabot Hamilton. My grandmother was very sick, close to death and had asked me to find his grave and give him her blessings before she parted this world.

I have been to the cemetery, but I don't know where his gravestone is. Could she please help me?

She said her name was Sister Maria and she would be happy to help. She said my grandmother must be very pleased to have such a fine grandson who would do this for her.

I mumbled something like "Yes, she's a wonderful lady" and followed the sister into a small dusty office cluttered with pamphlets, posters, and paraphernalia of Catholicism. There were dozens of statues of Jesus and the Virgin Mary and it smelled like an old trunk. In the corner was a card catalogue, like in a library, but smaller. She opened the drawer marked 'H'.

"Yes, here it is. Mr. Hamilton is interred in section 'L', plot 16." She unfolded a map from the top of the card catalogue, spread it out on her desk and pointed. "Lot 'L' is here, in the very far upper left-hand corner of the cemetery. You should have no trouble finding it." She handed me a pamphlet and patted me on the shoulder. It was the official brochure of the church. The bold title quote said, *Even though I walk through the darkest valley, I will fear no evil, for you are with me.* The pamphlet had a map of the cemetery. I thanked her and left, worried that my duplicity might cause the earth to open and suck me into its burning bowels.

I stopped for a sandwich at a local café and sat thinking, trying to figure out just what it was I was looking for. As I drove under the ivied arch, I had a dark sense of apprehension, as though I wasn't welcome there. I was not a part of this family, this community of souls. I didn't have any flowers to plant or prayers to offer—an interloper on a fool's mission, seeking guidance from a dead man. And I did fear evil, and was quite sure no one was with me who was going to make the fear disappear into the ether.

The weather was turning. The sun was setting, the sky turning grey, giving the gravestones an eerie darkness. A light snow had started to fall. I wanted to walk, to move my legs and arms, to breathe. I parked a few lots in, put the car facing the exit, just in case of anything, and began walking toward Lot 'L'.

A car drove in behind me, went up to the back of the graveyard, came down a few plots and parked. A man got out. A tall man in a blue parka and open-collared shirt. As I walked closer, it became clear the car was parked not near, but right in front of John Hamilton's tombstone. The man, suit jacket open, hands clasped behind his back, seemed to be looking at me, but I couldn't be sure of that because of the greying twilight and the sprinkling of snow.

I decided not to pay any attention to him. I walked right up to John Hamilton's gravestone. It was bigger than most, but not ornate. It said only — *John Cabot Hamilton* — *b. August 13, 1952* — *d. November 9, 2107.* *Devoted father, husband, friend and Patriot.*

His wife must have chosen those words, pointedly adding P*atriot* with a capital *P*. She's a tough cookie. I pretended to mutter a prayer or something to justify my presence. There wasn't anything else there that would point me in any beneficial direction and the man was still standing there, motionless, like a statue. I thought he might think it truly strange if I didn't say something to him, like, "Why are you staring at me?" or, more like Maggie, "Just what the fuck is your problem?"

I turned to him and said, "I have a map of the cemetery. Is there anything, some headstone or something, I can help you find?"

"No, thank you, I don't need any help."

"Oh, okay, I'm sorry."

The snow was gathering, the ground now white. Beside the stone was a short path leading to a patch of wildflowers. I walked beside the stone and down the path. There it was, at the end of his path! Just like he said, *follow me to the end of my path.* A grave plot cut into a small clearing in the weeds. I stumbled and jerked a bit, but there it was just as sure as a lightning bolt. Rule #10. *Do not Panic!* When the bear is coming after you, do not panic! Stay calm and act as if nothing had happened. Keep walking, slowly, do not falter!

I walked past the stone at the end of the path and turned back toward my car. I could feel the muscles in my neck and back tense. The effort to stay calm was sending shooting pains down both my arms. I dangled them and flopped them around a bit to try to loosen them, pretending I was trying to warm up. The snow was getting slippery underfoot. My guts twisted. I thought my knees might buckle.

A simple stone, no more than two feet tall and a foot wide and thin, a bargain basement thin grey slab, with words carved in a simple cursive — *M. S. Lynxe* — *b. 1992* — *d. 2016 Vox Clamantis In Deserto.*

Maybe he hadn't seen me react. My back was to him, not my face. I had jerked, I knew it. Maybe he hadn't seen that. Maybe saw me just stumble on a stone in the path. I tried to breathe normally but the air came into me in gasps and out of me in teeth-clenched gusts. Who was this guy? Was he still behind me? I didn't dare turn around.

I stopped and heard a footfall crunch in the snow on the path. I decided to walk on, walk on, walk on and get him as far away from his car as possible, then jump in mine and scream out of there. I fished the keys out of my pocket and put them in my right hand. Left hand door handle, right hand ignition. I could feel him closing. I was ten feet from my car and I dashed, grabbed the door handle, yanked it open, jammed the key in the ignition and twisted it to start. Then I looked up. He was standing right at the car, holding the door open. No smile, no frown, no nothing, like a face carved out of dense wood.

"Is your name Tobias?"

I slowly nodded.

"Do you have time for a cup of coffee?"

I nodded again.

"I'll meet you at the café down the road." He gently pushed my door closed and turned around, walking slowly away.

He held his coffee mug, nestled, as though to warm his hands. The wooden expression was gone. There were laugh-crinkles at the edges of his eyes and a softness about his mouth.

"I'm Jim Hatch. I'm married to John's sister. John and I have been close for twenty years. He had great respect for you. He told me that."

"That's nice. I appreciate that. Can I ask a couple of questions?"

"Sure."

"Why were you at the cemetery?"

"The week before John died, he spent a few days with us. I didn't see much of him. He would go off in the morning and do things, sometimes not coming back until late at night. But the day before he left, he said that if anything should happen to him, he wanted to be buried here, in Hudson, where he grew up. He said he had some enemies in law enforcement and asked me if I would keep an eye on his tombstone for a while—just to make sure nobody defaced it to slander his name." He sipped his coffee, looking off out the window. "He knew he was going to die. He wouldn't have said that if he didn't."

"So you asked Sister Maria to let you know if anyone came poking around, asking about his gravestone. So, she called you."

"Yes."

"Has there been anyone else 'poking around'?"

"No, you're the first."

I remembered John's wife telling the FBI guys that John's files burned up in his sister's barn. "Do you have a barn?"

"Yes, we do."

"Was there a fire there recently?"

"Funny you should ask. Someone else called about that a while ago. But no, there was a small fire in there, but that was about five years back. Why?"

"John had some papers that he didn't want anyone to find. He told people they burned up recently."

"Well, not in my barn. Nothing burned but a small patch of floor right in the middle of the entryway. Worker flicked a cigarette."

"Jim, what did John say about me?"

"He said you were a wonderful and tough young boy and if you came around, to help you out. I hope I have."

"You have, thanks." There was something else I had to know. Did he see me stumble and hear me gasp at Mary Sue's stone? "Are there any other gravestones, like friends or family, that John might have been visiting recently?"

"Well, his mother and father are buried there, same plot, but nothing else I know of."

I stood to go. He gave me a thank you and a quick embrace when we parted.

The trip back to Boston was going to be the hardest drive I had ever made. Slow and slippery with headlights and windshield wipers, a mind that raced back and forth, far and wide beyond the road in front of me. I grit my teeth … Found it! … Found it! … Found John Hamilton's files! … Probably….

If M.S. Lynxe was Mary Sue, then either Mr. Hamilton had used a marker that nobody in the world but me would ever understand or she really was buried there. The birth year was right, two years older than me and she had attended Dartmouth, if only for a few months. And her friend, the dumb sack of rocks, told Beanie she had died, been shot to death by a boyfriend. Maybe by some strange coincidence, it was her buried under that stone. Maybe the guy who shot her, if that's what happened, owned a family plot here.

I set the place to memory—Lot L-22. Before I dared do anything at all, I had to know if she was dead. Digging up the grave and prying open the casket was not an option if she was in it. That would be the end of the line for me. Either the rest of my life in jail or such serious mental problems that they would lock me in the nut house. I could ask Sister Maria who bought the grave lot, but that might eventually find its way from her to Jim, to the local coffee shop and to the local cops. Who knows?

If anyone put that connection together, the FBI would have no further use for me. On the upside, I had heard that law enforcement doesn't like to murder journalists. It causes problems. In my case, they would probably make an exception. I might, like the girls who were going to testify with John Hamilton, fall off a five-hundred-foot cliff or eat something that gave me a massive heart attack. I knew what I had to do, but before I could do it, I needed to shake the fear out of my bones and get my mind squared around, cleaned and washed, Buddhist-like. First, keep this car from going into a spin, into a mailbox, into a phone pole. Keep it straight.

16

AFTER GRADUATION, Bryce Haskell had been accepted into the Geisel School of Medicine, the Dartmouth medical school named after alumnus Theodore Geisel, the cartoonist and children's author, Dr. Seuss. He had told me he wanted to be a doctor, join Doctors Without Borders and travel the world administering care to people in high mountain regions who had no access to hospitals. He wanted to ski into their villages with his doctor's bag and magic medicines strapped on his back. It was snowing on the mountains and I knew, if he had a few days to plan, he would ski the mountain with me. There was something up there I needed to check out.

It was midnight when I got to Hanover. I checked into a local motel and asked the clerk to give me a wake-up call at seven. I sat on the bed thinking things through.

It seemed like there were two problems. First, Jim Lacey, who probably thought I believed he had murdered John Hamilton and then second, there were other guys, separate, who only wanted the files and thought I could lead the way to them. If I wasn't careful, that might happen and that was not what John Hamilton had wanted. I fell asleep watching late-night news coverage of a White House spokeswoman saying it was "absolutely, unequivocally" untrue that Donald Trump had engaged in sex with a porn star and no, the President had never said anything in support of white supremacists, "nothing, ever."

The Registrar's office in McNutt Hall opened at eight on the dot. Ethel Johnson had been the front desk secretary since before JFK was assassinated. She remembered me. That was sweet welcome. She took off her pink and black cat-eyes reading glasses, let them dangle from a gold chain around her neck, leaned closer, squinted, and said, "Well, good morning Tobias, what brings you here?"

I told her I was looking for two people — Bryce Haskell and Mary Sue Lynxe. When I said May Sue's name her eyebrows went up, her head tilted down and she gave me a top-of-the-eyelids stare. She apparently remembered the young girl's brief tenure at this august institution. I wondered what Mary Sue had done to make herself so memorable in such a short time. I didn't ask. I asked if there was a current address for her. Ms. Johnson pursed her lips, shook her head briefly and scanned her computer files.

"You are not the first person to ask for this address in the recent months."

"Who else asked for it?"

She slid her glasses down her nose and said, "You should know the privacy rules prohibit me from divulging that information."

I didn't know anything about any rules that might prevent her from answering that simple question, but I said, "Of course, I'm sorry."

"The address listed here is, 41 Glen Road, Pequot Falls, NH."

"Yes," I said, "but did she leave a forwarding address when she left?"

"That would be in a different file."

"Okay, do you have that file?"

"Tobias, do you really want to get involved with this girl?"

Wow, I thought, either she did really bad things in three short months or it is ivy league treason to be eighteen and show up pregnant, your bulge beginning to show.

"Ms. Johnson, I have no intention of getting involved at all."

"That would be wise. Here it is. #32 Rue Bisset, Sainte-Jeanne-d'Arc, Quebec, Canada."

"Oh, good, thank you." I wrote it down.

"You aren't planning on going there, are you?"

"No, oh gosh no, Ms. Johnson. A friend in Pequot Falls needs to get in touch with her concerning some documents. I offered to help by finding her address. That's all. And Bryce Haskell, do you have his address? He was my roommate here."

"I remember." More scrolling of files. "14 Blanchard Square. That's where a lot of Med students live. It's five or six blocks from here up North Main Street. It's winter vacation for them, but it's a long vacation. I hear almost none of them have left yet. Their study lamps are still on until two or three in the morning. Med school is very hard. Good luck to you, Tobias."

Walking the streets of Hanover brought me back to a time and place where I was young and comfortable, purposeful and sure of what I was doing. There was a morning crispness in the air, I could see my breath. I unzipped my jacket, stretched my arms and jogged a little, did a few of the exercises Bryce had taught me the first week of school more than four years ago. I smelled Starbucks a block away. I bought two regular coffees and four chocolate old fashioned glaze donuts — his favorite.

He looked exhausted at eight in the morning. He had been up most of the night studying the digestive system. Guts. He closed his worn-out edition of *Grey's Anatomy*. We hugged and talked about what we had been doing. Med school was much harder than he had thought it would be. It was brutal. I told him I was also having a rough time of it. I relayed most of the story of John Hamilton, saying nothing about the Sir John Motel or the files. It was safer for him if he didn't know.

"And I'm being followed around by the FBI. They think I know something that they don't know."

"Do you?"

"I think so. I haven't seen them since yesterday, so that's good. Maybe they stuck a tracking devise under my car. I don't know, and at this point I don't care."

"If that's all going on, Tobias, why are you here?"

"Because all I want to do is to ski the headwall on Mt. Washington. With you, if possible, before you go home to Alabama. I have to clear my mind. Get back to where I was and I'm not so sure I could make it on my own, either up or down. That's why. Can you do it?"

"Well, I have another day or two of studying that I have to get in and then two days before I fly home, so the answer is yes, my friend, I would love to jump the Ice Fall. Can you wait two days?"

"Absolutely. I will be back here on Wednesday evening. Can I crash here and then we go on Thursday morning? Does that work?"

"My roommates are both gone so I'll fix up a bed for you."

"I'll see you then." We hugged, and I left to go get my car and drive all day to Sainte-Jeanne-d'Arc, Quebec.

A couple of hours out of Hanover, I came to the Canadian border at Stanstead, Quebec. The officer took my passport, looked back and forth between me and the photo, swiped it, peered at his computer and picked up the phone. Minutes passed. A long line of cars were queuing up behind me. He put the phone down and waited. Minutes passed and then it rang. He picked it up, nodded and put it down.

"You are lucky today my friend. Bienvenue au Canada."

It was possible American authorities had posted my name at border crossings, and also possible that after things got ugly between the two countries, they said, "We're not honoring those requests today. Tough Luck, FBI." I headed toward Quebec City. I'd never been there but it was no time for sight-seeing. It was the time for driving and thinking.

The woman at the Sir John Motel might have been a pole dancer, but it was clear that wasn't all she was. She was at the pool with the mysterious Israeli guy. Maybe she's also a model and was there in England on a photo shoot. Maybe she worked for the government — one government or another. John Hamilton trusted her. He had given her the CD and my name. Somebody had to have figured out I was at that dive bar that afternoon. How would I have figured that out? I would have called Jasmine and asked her. She would have known that I was either there, around the corner at O'Rourke's, or at the South Ender. Somebody took those long-range telephoto videos. Who? Why? The FBI doesn't go around spying on people in Kiev, England and Red Square; the CIA does.

John Hamilton was probably shot by someone other than Tom Duncan, but without an autopsy or ballistics report it was only speculation, no way to prove it. The DA wouldn't give the gun back. That rifle had disappeared. The wrongful death suit, that might have disclosed the caliber of the entry wound, was dropped overnight. Just like that — yanked off the docket.

The Harvard professor seemed certain that Jim Lacey knew the answer and I was sure he wasn't going to tell anybody. He might even try to guarantee I wouldn't find out. The other feds, they only wanted the files and they wanted me to lead the way to them.

If Mary Sue Lynxe was alive in Quebec, or dead and buried up there, John Hamilton, associate director of the FBI, had hidden his files in an empty grave not more than fifty feet from his own tombstone. And he had talked to Beanie about her. He was FBI. He knew what had happened and where she was. Her gravestone with the Dartmouth motto was a road sign for me, and only me. Native Americans, he had said that snowy evening, call the lynx *the keeper of secrets*. How perfectly poetic.

By the time I approached Quebec City, all signs were in French. Past the city, there wasn't a trace of English. This was the heartland of the Quebecois, the native Canadians descended from French fur traders or the occasional Algonquian Indian. They wanted nothing to do with the Queen or her British Empire.

I came around a sharp curve on the narrow, two lane road and there was a moose standing on the pavement not more than twenty feet in front of me, unmoving. I swerved and went off the road, down a shallow embankment and, at thirty miles an hour, careened through a thick patch of high bush blueberries. I was stuck, only about ten feet off the road, but stuck. The car wasn't going anywhere. Neither was the moose. It just turned its giant head and stared at me. I had heard that a cow-moose is a very dangerous creature when there is a calf nearby, but I had to risk it. I needed to get onto the road to flag someone down.

A pick-up truck came, drove around the moose, pulled over. A young man my age and size got out, looked at my car, fished in the back of his truck, and dragged out a chain. The moose ambled across the road into the damp bushes. The man was bellowing cheery words in French and I didn't understand anything. He hooked it to his trailer hitch, fought his way through the bushes, and wrapped the chain around the frame of my car. He patted me on the shoulder and said something else. I could hear the gears grinding as he put it in four-wheel drive. He pulled the car up the embankment, onto the roadway, unhitched the chain, patted my shoulder again and drove away. I liked these people. The car seemed to run fine. No noises, no wobbles. Smooth.

The post office in Sainte-Jeanne-d'Arc was a single room on the side of the only gas station in town. A matronly woman of sixty or so was behind the counter sorting letters. I asked her where I might find #32 Rue Bisset. She gave me the same arched eyebrow look I had gotten from Ethel Johnson at the Registrar's office. She fished in a drawer, pulled out a map and with the eraser end of a pencil traced a path two blocks down, left, three blocks down, tapped it, folded up her map and said, *"Bonne chance."*

#32 Rue Bisset was a trailer, not a house — a mobile home with a long, tattered green awning along the front. The mailbox said, *Guimond.* I knocked. An old woman opened the door. She was old but still straight of bearing with white hair pulled into a ponytail. The skin on her face had only slightly wrinkled and it looked to me as though she had been quite beautiful in her youth.

She said, *"Bonjour, comment puis-je vous aider?"*

"My name is Tobias Starkey. I knew Mary Sue Lynxe in New Hampshire. I am in the area and thought I would stop by and say hello. Is she here?"

The woman turned to the house and hollered, *"Maurice, Benjoin, venez ici. Il y a un homme ici qui ne parle pa francais!"*

A man came through the living room holding the hand of a young boy. *Holy Shit!* I thought. He ducked his head as he walked under the ceiling light. The woman backed into the room and the man moved the boy in front of him putting his hands on the boy's shoulders. The boy said, in English, "What do you want?"

"My name is Tobias Starkey. I knew Mary Sue Lynxe in New Hampshire. I am in the area and thought I would stop by and say hello. Is she here?" The boy looked up at the man and translated to French.

The man said, "Non" and started to close the door.

I looked at the boy. I smiled and stood as tall and straight as I could. "Please, I don't need to talk to her. I just want to know if she is alive and well. I heard something had happened to her and I wanted to find out." That might have been exactly the wrong thing to say, but the boy and the man started talking, almost an argument.

Finally, the boy turned to me. His big brown eyes searched around my face. "Were you her friend?"

I was, at that moment, standing on the threshold both Mr. Hamilton and Ellen Pettigrew had warned me not to cross — "The truth is the truth. Always. Don't try to change it."

"No, not really. We lived in the same town. We knew some of the same people. She's two years older than me, but we went to the same college."

"What college?"

"Dartmouth."

"She told me about that. She was proud of it." He turned to the man and said something. The man, his eyes still wary, his body still braced in the doorway, relaxed his hands on the boy's shoulders.

They both walked past me, and the man took his hand again. They walked toward the woods. I followed.

We went along a path into the trees and came to a small graveyard bounded by an iron rail fence. There were six or eight markers, mostly simple stones but one was a granite cross with the carved words 'Marie Susan Lynxe.' Nothing more.

The boy stood in front of it, put his hand on one arm of the cross. "This is my mother. She is buried here. I miss her very much. She taught me English. She was a good mother." He began to softly cry. The man took his hand again and we walked back out of the woods. At the door, I asked the boy what his name was. Tears were still on his cheeks and his lip quivered. "This is Maurice Guimond, he is my uncle. My great-grandmother is Emma. My name is Benjoin, but my mother called me Beanie. I don't know why." The big man nudged the boy into the trailer, turned and gave me a glare that said, *If you ever come back, I will snap your neck like a dry twig.* The door closed, and the lockbolt snapped shut.

17

BEANIE WEEKS WASN'T BULLSHITTING. He knew just what he was talking about when he said, "That Mary Sue, she was the best piece of ass in this whole county. Bar none. Believe you me, I know." The question is, why did she do it? Was she actually attracted to him? Not likely. Did she want to find out what it was like to have sex with a one-legged man? Maybe. Did she have sympathy for him? Did she come to feel guilt for the loss of his leg, like she was responsible? She had flaunted her beauty, her face and the curves of her body in front of a poor, backwoods kid and he had maimed himself for life because of it. Give him a gift he would otherwise never have gotten. Most likely. She was Catholic, so probably good at the guilt thing, and had been accepted at Dartmouth, a special accomplishment she achieved with her mind, not her body. A triumph that was ripped from her bosom with a one-page expulsion notice. She would never have gone back to her parents in Pequot Falls, rejected and defeated, to marry Beanie Weeks. Nor ever have aborted her child. That, to her and to her family, would have been a violation of God's Grace. So, she went home to Quebec, to her grandmother, the strong and elegant grand-mère, Emma Guimond.

If gossip were true, she was shot by a boyfriend. That might be, or she died of cholera or got pregnant again by a brutal man she couldn't leave and shot herself. Or something that no one would ever talk about. In my mind, Mary Sue Lynxe was becoming an enigma.

Beanie didn't know he was the father of her child. The kid had said he didn't know why his mother called him Beanie. She had never told the boy who his father was. John Hamilton might have known. He must have been the other person asking the Registrar about Mary Sue after Beanie told him she went to Dartmouth, and then used his FBI connection to track her down.

I really wanted to see Maggie, but I wanted to first ski the bowl with my roommate and get my soul scrubbed. At nine at night, I pulled up to the American Customs and Immigrations checkpoint. I handed my passport to the officer. He swiped it, looked at his computer screen and asked, "Do you have anything to declare?"

"No, sir."

"Do you have any firearms, knives, explosives, tobacco or alcohol in your possession?"

"No, sir."

He handed my passport back. "Please pull over there," he said pointing to a parking spot in front of the immigration office. "You will be talking to Agent Donnelly. Ask for him at the desk. Your car may be searched while you are in the building, unless you request to be present. Do you?"

"No, sir."

"Leave your car unlocked, including the glove compartment and trunk. Proceed."

I didn't have to ask for Agent Donnelly. He met me at the door and ushered me into a small room. A room with a glass panel on the front. An interrogation room. A desk and two chairs. His computer. A ceiling light. Nothing else. He told me to empty all my pockets, put the contents on the desk and sit. I had only a few dollar bills, some change, my wallet, keys and passport. I put them on the desk.

He opened the wallet and glanced in it, folded it shut and put it back on the desk. He made no comment of the hundreds of dollars in the wallet. My steno pad was in the glove compartment. I had taken no notes about this trip and had never spelled out anyone's name. I used only initials. None of it would mean anything to them.

He picked up my passport. These guys, unlike other law enforcement people, seemed to have absolute power to do anything they wanted. I wondered whether I was in the United States, whether I had the rights and privileges enumerated in the Constitution. No, clearly, I didn't. I hadn't yet passed through the Point of Entry. I was in a special zone that some law had designated as exempt from such things as unreasonable search and seizure, due process and all the other things millions of Americans had died to create and defend. Nope, I wasn't home yet. I was somewhere else. A nowhere land. I wondered why I was there. What had flagged me?

He swiped my passport on his computer. "Mr. Starkey, you entered Canada at 11:24 this morning. Now, at 9:15 this evening, you are leaving. That's quite a short trip. Where did you go?"

"I went to the town of St. Joan of Arc."

"And what did you do there?"

"I went to the home of Emma Guimond."

"I see. Did you bring anything into Canada that you left behind?" He leaned hard forward and put his eyes right in mine.

His question meant he thought I might have smuggled drugs or something, sold them and left. That was a relief. They hadn't known where I went, who I was looking for or why I was there. That wasn't what flagged me. It might have been that such a short stay would flag anybody. Or maybe just a general notice that listed, among others, a Tobias Starkey.

"No sir, I didn't bring anything into the country, didn't sell or buy anything. I just went to see some people who live there."

"Who is that?"

"Emma Guimond." Everybody says you should only answer the exact question and offer no more information, but I thought if I gave him a brief and plausible explanation it might stop him from boring down deeper, asking questions that might force me to lie. "I knew her granddaughter. We went to the same college. I had a couple of days off. I wanted a short road trip. I decided to go there and say hello. She wasn't there. The grandmother didn't speak a word of English and I don't speak a word of French, so I left."

He looked at his computer screen. "You're a journalist. Is that right?"

The application for a passport includes a description of your profession, such as: politician, sex-trafficker, oligarch, spy, journalist; he already knew the answer.

"Yes, sir, that's correct."

"Are you writing a story?"

"I don't know. I doubt a one-day road trip to Quebec where nothing happened would make it past an editor."

"Maybe this stop here at the border might catch their attention." He smiled. It was not a friendly smile.

"That's a thought, but too many people are already doing that and they're doing it for political purposes. There's nothing political here. I just took a trip and you're just doing your job. No, it's sad, but it wouldn't get published. No dirt."

A uniformed woman knocked on the window. I turned around. She poked her head into the room. She seemed excited.

"Agent Donnelly, we have a probable 212."

"Canine unit?"

"Positive, sir."

"Mr. Starkey, thank you, you're free to go."

"Agent Donnelly, do you know where there is a cheap motel nearby? I'm beat."

"Get off the highway at Rte. 5. Go toward Derby. There's one motel still open this time of year. It's not far. Couple miles. Real cheap."

I shouldn't have felt so confident so soon. As I left, I turned around and saw him on the phone. It was possible the FBI or CIA—or whatever spooks were dogging me—had left an advisory with Border Controls and other law enforcement agencies around the country. Precautionary. Nothing specific because he let me go. Just a request for notification. Now they were being notified. Once again, they knew where I was. But the agent was all of a sudden busy now with a 212, canine positive.

Neither the FBI nor the CIA could ever find the files without knowing two things—that Mary Sue Lynxe of Pequot Falls got pregnant by a one-legged boy, went to Dartmouth, got kicked out, moved to Canada, had the child, died and was buried. That Beanie Weeks was the father might not have been important, but to me, it was central. It was why she would never be found in Pequot Falls. John Hamilton was fascinated by the story and the name 'Lynxe' as *the keeper of secrets*. Nobody on earth, but me, knew those two things.

Also, I was certain that Maurice Guimond was not going to let anybody do again what I had done, no matter what uniforms they were wearing. He didn't like that at all. He was a very big man and he had not been happy. He wanted his cousin to rest in peace and her child, his now, to be left alone. Grand-mère Emma would answer the door and call Maurice. He would remand the child to his room and go alone to speak with them. His body would fill the entire doorway and he would say, "Non." And then he would say, "Non," again and that would be it.

Perhaps, Emma herself would talk to them. The door would shut more graciously, more slowly, but the snap of the lock would be even more firm and final. The dots were too far apart, too random. I was the only one who could see them in a sequence.

The motel was low, low budget. Not as bad as the Sir John, but not even one whole star. Maybe a half because the guy at the office counter was nice, polite and almost as big as Maurice Guimond. Boy, were people large in these northern climes. Nor were razor blades a big selling item around here.

He gave me a room at the far end. There was only one other car in the lot. I gave him thirty bucks cash and that was good with him. There was a bar down the road about a quarter mile. I unpacked in the room, zipped up my jacket and set off on foot. The cool air on my face and in my lungs brought my back up straight and a smile all to myself on the dark and quiet road.

Tough Thyme's Bar and Grill had a long counter, pool table, music station and a few booths. A handful of men were at the bar. A couple of punk kids were at a booth—shaved heads, tattoos and teeth missing. The place was quiet. Murmuring talk. A guy was eating a cheeseburger, so I ordered one and a Budweiser. It was quiet for a bar.

I'd just finished my cheeseburger and a second beer when a woman came into the bar. She was in civilian clothes, pants, sneakers, checked flannel shirt and a light jacket, but it was the woman who poked her head into the interrogation room with the 212 alarm. I was sure of it. She came in, looked around, looked right at me, and left.

The menu had said five bucks for the cheeseburger, three apiece for the beer. I put fifteen on the counter, walked to the door, looked down the road and saw a car, a quarter mile down the road, pull into the motel. I set off at a full-bore run.

When I got to the edge of the driveway, she was coming out of the office, walking toward my car. I hunkered down in the trees and watched. She got a coat out of her front seat, folded it, went to my car and opened the rear door. Shit! When was I ever going to learn to lock my car? She put the coat on the back seat and then did something else. She was bent over hard, rummaging around, she seemed to be pulling and pushing, then straightened up, closed my door and went back to her car. I crawled low into some bushes and waited until she was gone.

I am wearing my jacket. That is not my jacket in the back seat of my car. The office man smiled when I went in.

"I thought I saw someone put something in my car. Did anyone come in here and talk to you about that?"

"Yes, it was an Immigration Officer. She said you had left your coat at their office when you passed through today and she lived nearby and was returning it to you. She was very nice. She showed me her badge."

"Did she say how she knew I was here?"

"Yeah, she said you told the agent-in-charge you had planned to come here."

"Ah, yes, so I did. That was very nice of them. I was wondering where that jacket went. Thank you for letting her do that."

"Sure, but really I didn't have much choice. She had that badge and that means she can do anything she wants and that was what she wanted to do. She was clear about that. I didn't even ask her to leave it with me, which I would've done with anyone else. Those people are not anyone else."

"Anyway, thank you, Glad to have my jacket back. You here all night?"

"No, I get off at eleven, back tomorrow at three. Six days a week. Fifty weeks a year, three years and counting."

So, what was she doing rummaging around in my back seat? Planting a bomb so when the car moves, I get blown to Kingdom Come? No, they don't want me dead because then they lose. Except Jim Lacey, he probably does want me dead. He might think I can prove he shot John Hamilton. But all the other guys, they need me. I'd get the jacket, search it and check out my back seat in the morning when a different person is in the office.

The jacket was a jacket. Nothing in it. No torn stiches, no lumps. Just a jacket like any other. It had been a ruse to get her into the car. To do something that they hadn't had time to do at the border crossing because they got quick-like wound up in a 212, with dogs. Agent Donnelly had called some office and they told him to do something, but I had already gone on down the road.

The morning was clear and bright. Still only one other car in the parking lot. I searched the seat cushions, deep down in the crack between them, along the side and down in the seat belt hole. She hadn't leaned in far enough to get to the middle. I took the floor mat out, shook it. Nothing. The sub-mat was glued to the metal floor, but a corner was loose. I pulled it up and there was a flat, round, black, skinny rubber disc with a round lump in the middle stuck to the metal by a ring of thin magnets. It wasn't going to be a bomb—

I'd already figured that out. It had to be a GPS transmitter. I pulled it out, walked over to the other car in the parking lot, got down on my belly, out of sight of the office, and stuck it on the frame. Hope they had good travels and met interesting people.

I wanted to feel the warmth of Maggie's skin spread over my chest. I wanted to hear her laugh, boss me around, make fun of me, to feel her feline sinews wrap me tight on my narrow bed. To take her back to Mama D's. Soon I would do all of that. First, ski the headwall — clear my mind and look to see if there was any evidence that the top of that mountain was the end of John Hamilton's path—that it might be where he had left his file. I didn't think it possible that he could have or would have. He didn't have time and it wouldn't have made any sense, but I had to check.

Then to find my girlfriend, hold her close and ask her to help me one more time. I needed her to ask a question that I couldn't ask. If it were me, standing there, phrasing the simple request, all the dots would line up for someone else to see. I couldn't risk that. I needed Maggie, or someone, not me, to ask Sister Maria who secured the burial plot for Mary Sue Lynxe. Then I could get to one-hundred percent certain that I was going to find a moonless winter's night and rob a grave.

18

BRYCE'S APARTMENT BUILDING had a shared kitchen and lounge with a TV. While he finished his studying, I sat, sipping a beer, watching the news. Christmas was coming in a week, but none of the stories were about the birth of Christ. They were all, in one way or another, about Donald Trump. His National Security Advisor, Michael Flynn pleaded guilty to charges of lying to the FBI and Justice Department about his contacts with Russians. Why would he be dumb enough to lie? A new tax bill was passed pushing money upward to the already rich. Federal protections of the Utah National Monuments were cut back paving the way for corporate extraction of fossil fuels on two million acres. Omarosa Manigault, the most senior black woman in the Trump administration, resigned, or, they speculated, had been forced out or fired. Another school shooting. This one in New Mexico. Another disturbed white kid who liked Hitler shot to death two Hispanic students.

The president said, "My administration is determined to do everything in our power to protect the students and keep weapons out of the hands of those who pose a threat to themselves and others."

There was an ominous pattern emerging. Mr. Hamilton had said that all Trump cared about was himself and his money. He had won the election with the support of angry white men and foreign actors.

How do you get the most people possible to love you, adulate you, and at the same time take all their money and give it to rich people? Develop a cult of personality where no matter what you do or say, your base will love it because you did it or said it. They won't know what you did or what you said or how it affects them. They won't care. They only care about you. Deport as many brown-skinned people as possible. Build a wall to keep the rest out. Stall justice reform to keep black people in jail. Refuse to denounce white supremacy. Stoke the fires of the racial divide and give your people as many guns as they want. Move all the money to white corporate America and break century-old bonds with allies who give money to support their poor and allow Arabs and Africans through their borders. Tell your people the reason they've suffered is because of 'fake news' and 'deep state' actors, whoever they are, and say it over and over and over again. The collective mind will numb. No matter how blatant the lie, repeat it endlessly — soon they will swallow it hook, line and sinker. Pure fiction will become the truth. Make it all about you. Embrace the Russians, the North Koreans, the Israelis. Why them? What's the plan? Are you in charge of this plan, or is somebody else? Are you just a pawn in a much bigger game? A complete global realignment?

There was one really big thing I didn't get. Why was it that Evangelical Christians loved this man? He was thrice married, an adulterer many times over. No question about that. Probably had sex with porn stars. Evangelicals, as far as I knew, didn't like porn stars or the men who had sex with them. Every day, every night, late into the night, he said repulsive, demeaning and hateful things about innocent people. Sure, they were usually dark-skinned people, but wasn't the Lord Jesus Christ a savior who opened his arms and heart to the poor and dispossessed? And wasn't he a dark-skinned man himself? Why were these Evangelicals so happy to forsake their faith, the teachings of their Lord for this man? What was Donald Trump giving them that was more powerful than their own faith? That buffaloed me.

When I went to bed, I was depressed and frightened about that and about what I might find in Mr. Hamilton's files. If I found them.

We stopped in Pequot Falls to get my skis, boots, poles and a pint bottle of brandy to celebrate after we made our run down the mountain. Bryce was quiet, taciturn; his mind still deep inside the mysteries of the intestinum duodenum.

"Bryce, leave it behind for a day. Let's ski and feel good about everything."

"Okay, you're right. What do you want to talk about?"

"Uh, politics? No. Religion? No. Sex, how about sex?"

Bryce said, "No, I can't remember anything about it."

We rode in silence to the base camp in Pinkham Notch. The parking lot was nearly empty — a couple of Park Service trucks and four other cars were parked behind the lodge. I parked the car by a sign that said, *Concord Coach Line to Boston — Departs here at 8:45AM — Departs Wildcat Mt. Lodge at 9:00AM.*

Over the treetops, I could see the bowl from half-way up to the rim. I couldn't see the bottom—too many trees. It looked stark and lonely up there. We strapped our skis and poles on our backs and began the climb. The park rangers had busted out the trail to their cabin with their skimobiles. Two hours in and we reached the camp. It was a mile to the east of Tuckerman Ravine, on a sloping shoulder of the mountain. It was built out of the path of avalanches, so the rangers would survive to help the lost or injured. We unstrapped our skis and stomped out our boots on the stoop.

Someone inside yelled, "Come on in." Two rangers were sitting by a wood stove, drinking coffee.

"Good morning," I said, "I'm Tobias Starkey. I'm a journalist from Boston. This is my friend, Bryce Haskell. He's a med student at Dartmouth. We were here a couple of months ago with John Hamilton. We skied the bowl with him. It was fantastic. We're here to do it again in his memory. He died a month ago in a hunting accident."

"Yeah, I heard about that. That is really sad. John was a good man and a good lawman. He had a great sense of humor and didn't like people who were all full of themselves. A real loss."

"Yes, I agree. I spent a lot of time with him growing up. He was a mentor to me, a real friend."

"Well you kids should have the mountain to yourselves. You're the first to pass by. The lodge radioed that there was one other skier on his way up behind you, but that's it. There is a huge amount of snow up above the bowl, so watch the snowpack above.

We climbed the same path we had climbed before, digging hand holes and pushing on toe holds on the steeper sections, pushing with poles where the angle of ascent allowed. It was clear — no fog on the mountain. The sun was mid-morning high. The air cold and fresh. I could see my breath with every exhale. It was another two hours to the rim. We settled into a rhythm, one hand, one foot, pull and push, the other hand, the other foot, pull and push. Bryce was ahead so I could use his divots and match his pace. I had made it before. I knew I could make it again. I didn't worry that he was not behind me. I didn't even think about it, just pulled and pushed in a steady climb. We made good time. In an hour and a half, I could see the rim above.

Bryce reached the rim, scrambled over, dug his heels in, and gave me a hand. We were two thousand eight hundred feet above the roof of the lodge where we started. The summit loomed two thousand feet above us, white and muscular.

I told Bryce to hold on a minute. There was something I had to check. I had wanted to come here because of something Mr. Hamilton had said when we were here together: "At the end of every path, one danger is behind and another is ahead." Follow the path all the way to the end, he had also told me.

The rock out-cropping, the 'scarp' as Mr. Hamilton had called it, was still visible. I walked over to it, got down as close to the granite crevices as I could, and inspected every inch of it. There was nothing there. This was not where he had hidden his file. We put our skis on and skied back and away from the lip. We could see all the options for descent — the four Gulleys, the Chutes, Icefall and Sluice.

"Which one did Toni Matt run?" I asked.

"I don't know, that was before they had any names for them."

"Then let's go down the way we went before."

"That's the Icefall. It's right in front of us."

We pulled our hats tight on our heads, zipped our parka collars up over our throats, made sure our gloves were snug, and slid our goggles over our eyes.

To our left, a hundred feet away, back beyond the edge of the snowpack in a protected bowl, a man was standing at the top of the rim. He had just climbed over the lip. His skis were still on his back, his coat was unzipped. He wasn't wearing a hat or goggles. He was tall with close-cropped hair. He took a few steps toward us. He had a limp. It was Jim Lacey. The FBI agent. I was sure of that. He reached inside his coat and pulled out a pistol and raised the barrel.

I slammed Bryce on the back with my pole and screamed, "Gun, Go, Go!"

We both lunged at the same instant. The stillness in the air, and the dense wall of snow just behind us, made the sound of the pistol shot a loud, clean, crack. I didn't hear a second shot. If there was one, it's sound was drowned by the mighty rumble of a million-ton beast freed from her moorings on the rock above. Avalanche!

I went over the lip full-bore and left the mountain, flying. Bryce was ahead of me. Maybe I was up there for a minute, maybe ten seconds, but in that space, all time dissolved. I was there forever, seeing the man pull his gun to shoot us dead, hearing the avalanche break free and roar, knowing it was coming behind us, trying to catch us, to crush us, swallow us and bury us on this brutal mountain.

"Mt. Washington," I had said to Bryce when he asked what mountain I liked to ski.

"Wow!" he had said. "An alpine guy. That's totally cool."

The ground was coming up fast. I watched Bryce lean forward over his skis as far as he could, tuck in his poles, lean into it, keep the tips up. Up! Lean! I rocked my heels back as far as I could, and the tails of my skis hit the surface. I began to shake and went into a wobble. Ski tips down. Don't fall or you're dead. Stop the wobble. I was going much too fast to get my poles out or turn at all. I saw Bryce crouch low and shoot like a bullet down through the throat of the headwall. I tucked and crouched and followed him down. The noise was a thunder of snow and a scream of wind.

My wobble was gone as I passed the end of the bowl but the whole of the ground was shaking under my skis. The slope became shallower. I could feel a slowing and the surface became solid again. I saw trees a thousand feet ahead, I saw Bryce ease up out of his crouch, plant a pole and give a sideward nudge to his skis. I did the same and soon we were able to wiggle the tails of our skis side to side, to take control, slow down enough to get into the trees without crashing.

I followed him through the woods to a clearing above the lodge. We looked back. It was silent. There was no bowl on Mt. Washington. It was a rounded face of snow to the edge of the rock above. The summit was clear, grey granite in a blue, cloudless sky. The surface of the snow still rippled, and the air above was full of white shimmering crystal.

With just barely enough of a head start, we'd outrun the avalanche over the Icefall, straight down the mountain through Tuckerman Ravine to the bottom four miles away in Pinkham Notch. We hugged; a hard, close hug, but one without a sound. We were still too terrified to speak or even smile. Jim Lacey, that murderous agent, was probably at the rim, smiling to himself.

Bryce turned to ski to the lodge. I grabbed his sleeve.

"No, I can't go there. I have to be dead."

In my mind, I heard the questions from the rangers and then the reporters—*Was there another man up there? Did you see him? What do you think triggered the avalanche?* And my answers would have had to be—*I don't know, I didn't see anybody*. Or the questions would never end and the FBI, or whomever has been watching me, would know I was lying and be all over me like a dog on a bone. I would never find those files, or worse, I would, and they would pounce on me before my fingers even touched them, and then I would be dead — for real.

I knelt in the snow, concentrating hard.

"Bryce, listen really carefully to me. I jumped the lip first and you saw me fall at the bottom of the bowl. You couldn't stop. You were going ninety miles an hour and the avalanche was right behind you touching the tail of your skis. I'm back up there buried under a mountain of snow. This is important. I have to be dead."

"Why?"

"It's complicated. You don't want to know."

"Why would they believe that I made it and you didn't?"

"Because you are a world-class skier, and I'm not. You had a shot at it and you made it. I didn't have any chance at all."

"Was that guy trying to shoot us?"

"I don't know, maybe he was just making sure an avalanche took us out."

"Who was he?"

I looked at my friend and shook my head.

He also knelt. We could only see the roof of the lodge, so they couldn't see us. Nobody could.

"What if somebody saw us both come all the way down?"

"From the lodge and parking lot, you can only see the top of the bowl, remember? Too many trees to see the bottom. That's why you need to tell them I fell half-way down. That's where nobody could see me."

"Okay, I'll do this. After I'm done talking to everybody, I'll pick you up on the road down here."

"No, it's too risky. What if there is an accident, or a roadblock for drunk drivers? Anything could happen. If any cop finds me and finds that you have lied, we're both cooked. Take my mother's car, be sure to tell them you're taking it, and go back to Dartmouth."

It was afternoon. I could hear a hubbub of cars and people down below us. Police were coming, reporters were coming. I could hear the ranger's snowmobiles coming down the trail.

"You got to get going." I said. "Don't worry about me. I know how I'm getting back."

I bowed down my head, finding the will power to concentrate. Who do I trust? Maggie, Bryce, Ellen Pettigrew, and maybe, maybe Alice Turnbell.

"Do me a favor—in the trunk of the car is a blanket, my hiking boots and my hunting knife. In the glove compartment is my note pad. Could you put all that stuff in a bag and throw it up in the woods where no one can see it, maybe, let's say, five phone poles down the road from the lodge? I'll find it."

"That's it?"

"No. When you get Dartmouth, after all the reporters are done with you, call Ellen Pettigrew and tell her that I'm alive and fine and I'll call her at her office tomorrow at two in the afternoon. I have to ask her to do a favor for me. Tell only her, nobody else. Good luck, Bryce, and thank you."

He was quiet for a moment. "That had to be less than six minutes."

"Definitely. Toni Mott move over."

He touched my cheek with his gloved hand, stood, and skied off into the beehive below.

19

IN NORTHERN NEW HAMPSHIRE, in late December, the sun sets in mid-afternoon. At the foot of Mt. Washington, on the eastern slope, the light is gone by four. The cold descends into the valley and the air, down in the lee of a ridge, becomes still. The chatter of day creatures, small birds and squirrels, is gone. The hoots of the owls and yips of the coyotes begin. The snow is harder, less giving.

I had to get to a place a mile through the woods, near where Bryce would throw a bundle up over the snowbank. There were no paths. Old growth and new growth made a thicket too dense to ski through. I put my skis and poles on my back and began to trudge through knee-deep snow, counting phone poles along the road.

The bus to Boston left from the Visitor's Center in the morning, but I couldn't risk being seen by rangers as I bought a ticket inside the lodge. I was going to have to make it to Wildcat Mountain lodge by nine in the morning. It was only a couple miles away, but it was through the forest in the dark. I'd never make it in this darkness.

The fifth pole was at the foot of a steep embankment. On the top of the rise above it was a small plateau. It looked as though it had been cleared four or five years ago. Now, it was forested with small, new growth pines, only eight or ten feet tall. The trunks were the size of baseball bats and the branches, thin with soft, pale green needles, went to the ground. It was a serene little place. I bent a trunk over to see if it snapped. It didn't. It was supple, and the wood looked soft. Back a few feet from the edge of the slope, behind a few trees, I cleared a space to sit, broke some branches, and made a dry seat of pine boughs.

A few cars went by. None slowed down. Then two police cruisers. After their taillights had disappeared around a bend in the road, my mother's car came slowly, and pulled to a stop by the phone pole.

Bryce jumped out, ran around to the passenger's side, pulled out a large, black bag, and heaved it up over the snowbank into a gulch at the foot of the slope, out of sight of the road. He didn't look around. He didn't wait. He jumped back in the car and drove off south to Dartmouth.

I sat on my pine needle cushion wondering how it had gone for Bryce. It couldn't have been easy. In all the years I had known him, he had never lied, never even exaggerated. Now, he had had to do that, not for himself, he wouldn't have done that, but for me. I waited for dark to come, when all the cars would have their headlights on and I could see them coming for a long stretch of road.

Somewhere in that waiting, the enormity of the avalanche, of the blind race caught up with me—the pistol shot, sailing through the air, the wobble, the shaking ground, the scream of the wind and the roar of snow chasing me, trying to catch me, to kill me—and I began to shiver. I wasn't cold, zipped in my goose-down parka. As I sat alone in that unfamiliar wood, I was terrified, not of what was going to happen, not of what was happening, but of what had already happened. And I shivered, overpoweringly, until I began to shake, just as the ground underneath had shook, and I began to weep. I wept as I hadn't wept since I was a child; fat, alone and sure that no one loved me. And now my mother was gone off to some Godforsaken place. She left me without a tear. My government had murdered my friend and then, up here, on the cold ridge of that mountain, they had tried to murder me. I wiped my tears, washed my face with snow, and stared off into the sky thinking about Maggie. I had wanted her to help me, but now it was more important that she believed I was dead. They might still be watching her. That's why I asked Bryce to get in touch with Ellen Pettigrew.

A car came by with its headlights on. Then another. I eased to the edge of the embankment. Nothing in either direction. I slid down to the gulch, grabbed the bag and scrabbled my way back up, swinging the bag behind me, trying to wipe my footprints off the slope.

On top everything in the bag was a note — *Presentation went well. Only lasted five minutes. We got our license and a $3,000 down payment through Visa. 6693. Call me when you get back from Corpus Christie.* That's right, doctors and lawyers study Latin. What a careful friend. No signature. What did he mean, *We got our license?* And $3,000 through Visa? 6693; his ATM code. There must be a license and a credit card in here somewhere. I put the note in my mouth and chewed it to a pulpy wad and spit if off into the trees.

The hiking boots had a dry pair of wool socks in them. I realized how hard-soled and cold the ski boots were. I changed. My feet felt snug and warm. Twenty feet back in the woods, I dug a deep trench in the snow and buried my skis, poles, goggles, boots and used socks. By the time anyone found them, it wouldn't matter. I would be, like Lazarus, like Christ himself, back from the dead. I slid the knife and sheath onto my belt. In the blanket was the pint of brandy, a rolled-up belly pack, and the first aid kit that he always carried in his backpack, just like a good doctor would. In with the bandages and ointments were a toothbrush and a comb. My notes, his driver's license and his Visa card were slid into the Band-Aid box. They were wrapped in a plain piece of paper that bore his signature in pen. I put them both it in my wallet.

With the knife, I began to cut the boughs to build a little hut, just like John Hamilton had taught me in the woods behind his house ten years ago. A shelter that I could crawl into and try to sleep through the night. I had to build it before total darkness set in, before I couldn't see which branch to cut or how to weave them into a shallow arch, then pile boughs thick enough to keep the night air from falling in on me. Darkness came as I piled snow on top to hide it from view and keep whatever warmth I had inside my hut. The opening was two feet tall and three feet wide. It was long enough so my head wouldn't stick out. It was beautiful. I opened the bottle of bandy and drained about half of it down my throat, then slithered in backwards on my belly, feet first.

I don't know how many parts the human mind, body and spirit have, all combined, but when I wrapped myself in my blanket, took another slug of brandy, and put my head on my pillow of soft pine needles, every one of them was exhausted, worn through to their last thread.

I was still on my belly when the squawking bark of a blue jay woke me. Skinny fingers of light filtered through the pines. The sky was yellow-orange with early light.

With hands and elbows, I crawled out. It was cold. Far below freezing. As the sun rose, it would warm a bit, but not much. I took off my wool hat, unzipped my parka, and washed my face with snow, brushed my teeth with snow, combed my hair, put my hat back on, zipped the parka, and cut a slice open in the middle of the blanket. I slid my head through the slit. The blanket became a poncho, cinched at the waist by the belly pack in the back. I threw the brandy bottle as far as I could. It disappeared deep in the snow. The hut easily collapsed. When the snow was smoothed out over the top, it was gone.

I checked my watch. It was just past six. I had about two hours to get two miles through the woods to the lodge at the base of Wildcat Mt., eat something, get a ticket and get on the bus to Boston.

In the quiet of the morning, I couldn't hear any cars or see any headlights either way. The snowbank at the bottom of the slope was hard, dirty and crusty. My feet hit it with a jolt. I climbed over, crouched, sprinted across the road, dove over that pile and rolled into the scrub. Stay out of sight, Always Know Where You Are. Don't Get Lost in the Woods. I didn't have a compass to help find my way back, so I had to keep the road in sight. Mr. Hamilton had taught me how to use my wristwatch as a compass — *point the hour hand at the sun. Halfway between there and 12 is approximate south.* But the sun wasn't up yet, and he had said 'approximate' was being generous. It depended on your latitude. Maybe good for general direction over long distances, but worthless for short hikes.

Burying my skis was the right choice. The woods were too dense to ski through. The going was slow, the snow nearly knee-deep. With the parka and poncho, I was warm. I would bury the blanket before I got to the lodge and walk in like an early morning hiker. There must be a lot of those up near these resorts. Vigorous city people who get up at the crack of dawn, put on a thousand dollars' worth of specialty cloths and gear, and bound out of their B & B for a morning constitutional through the unspoiled wilderness. They had smart phones to tell them where the trails were, whether it was going to snow and what bear scat looked like and where south actually was. I didn't have one of those. I didn't know where the trails were, but I hoped I would show up looking just like one of them, all bushy-tailed and rosy-cheeked, ready to talk Pileated Woodpeckers, spruce cones, bear markets or whatever it was they talked about.

It was past eight when the lodge came in sight. The parking lot was nearly full. I took off my hunting knife, kissed it, told it what a good friend it had been, wrapped it in the blanket and buried them.

I walked onto the pavement, shaking my arms and jogging a little bit, looking vigorous. There was only a short line at the ticket counter. Everyone who was buying a ticket had to show identification. That's what Bryce knew. Post 911 Patriots Act. I took out his card and waited my turn. He and I looked enough alike and were about the same size so if I kept my hat on it would probably be okay.

Her name tag said, *Zoe*.

"Boston South Station, one way." I handed the girl Bryce's license. She looked at it, typed something into her computer and handed it back.

"That will be $32.50."

I gave her Bryce's credit card. She swiped it and it went through. I signed his name, thanked her and took the ticket.

"Are there newspapers for sale here?"

"No, not here. They give them out for free on the bus. You can get one there."

I went to the breakfast buffet table. There were a lot of healthy-looking trail-hikers sipping latte and eating organic nuts and bananas. I fixed a plate of scrambled eggs, bacon, sausage, potatoes, English muffins and a large black coffee. I thought of Maggie. She could eat two of these.

When Zoe reads the paper, she's going to say, "Wow, the guy who raced the avalanche and beat it was here today. I sold him a ticket to Boston. That's cool. Can't wait to tell Bob." Instead of,

"Wow, the guy who died in the avalanche was here today. I sold him a ticket to Boston. That's not cool. I better tell Bob." Thank you, my friend.

The state-wide paper, the *Union Leader,* ran the article on the front page. ***Skier Dead in Avalanche on Mt. Washington.*** It was a thorough piece, distributed through Associated Press, so the *Globe* had it also. Dead in the avalanche: Tobias Starkey of South Boston, 24-year-old journalist with the *Boston Globe.* His companion, Bryce Haskell of Strupps Corner Alabama, 24-year-old first year medical student at the Geisel School of Medicine, Dartmouth College outran the massive avalanche and made it safely to the bottom of the mountain He was a flat-out hero, a skier of incredible strength and bravery. He was so deeply saddened by loss of his friend and former roommate and wished he could have stopped and helped him down the mountain. Me not so much a hero. I hadn't made it. I died. They didn't expect to find my body until spring melt. That section of the mountain would be closed until the remains could be safely retrieved for proper burial.

It all seemed to confirm that Jim Lacey had not died on the mountain. He was off too far beyond the rim. He must have known that. His car would have been left in the parking lot. They didn't say anything about that. The article didn't mention him at all. It didn't say anything about a pistol shot.

I'm sorry, Maggie, I'll see you as soon as I can. They would have asked the *Globe* who my next of kin was. Jasmine would have steered them to Maggie and she would have told them—there was only one, a mother who was a few miles south of the North Pole in some place where there were no newspapers, phones or internet, only walruses and bearded seals. So, they published my name. I was more than just dead; I was *officially* dead.

Harvard Square is six stops on the Red Line from South Station. The square was quiet. Most students were gone for Christmas vacation. I bought a *Globe* at the news stand on the corner by the Harvard Coop. It was the same AP article as the local paper had run. This article, however carried a quote from Sam Borstien at the bottom of the article, saying what a fine young journalist I was and how their thoughts and prayers went out to my family. At least he didn't have to fire me now, unless he already had and neglected to inform his readers of that fact. Fortunately, there was no file photo of me.

Alice Turnbell was on vacation. The security guard looked at me a little suspiciously, then waved. The passcodes she had given me worked. Both the outer door and the door to her office opened. The computer on her desk fired up and her password opened access. There wasn't one piece of paper anywhere. At the end of the sofa were folded blankets, sheets and a pillow. What a sweet woman. I had some time before I called Ellen Pettigrew at Dartmouth. I decided to begin my article — to get the first paragraph down so I knew where I was going.

John Cabot Hamilton was one of the most senior law enforcement officials in the government. He was the Associate Director of the FBI for Counterintelligence and National Security. On November 7, 2017, Mr. Hamilton was shot to death in a hunting accident in Pequot Falls, New Hampshire. A young man named Tom Duncan, 22, of Pequot Falls, said he mistook him for a deer. The state Fish & Game Department agreed with the young man's account. He was charged with 'negligently shooting a human being while hunting', pled nolo contendere in court, was fined five hundred dollars and had his hunting license suspended for ten years. The case was closed within a month of Mr. Hamilton's death.

There had been no investigation of this death submitted to the court prior to the sentencing.

Was this an unfortunate hunting accident? Is that what really happened? A review of documentary evidence strongly suggests that something very different may have occurred on that drizzly November morning high in the mountains of northern New Hampshire.

I ended it with this statement:

John Cabot Hamilton was shot through the back and neck five days before he was to testify, behind closed doors, to a Senate Committee investigating Russian interference in the 2016 presidential election. He, and he alone, had documents which detailed events dangerously undermining the very foundation of American Democracy. He had not shared these documents with any other agency — the CIA, the NSA, or even his boss, James Comey, the Director of the FBI for fear that the documents might find their way into the hands of government officials with a political agenda and disappear forever. He wanted to share them only with elected officials in the United States Senate. John Hamilton believed in the Constitution of the United States and believed that Article One, establishing Congress as the first body of three, was the most important arbiter of truth. I know that. He told me that. He was a close friend of mine. Two other people, both women, also scheduled to testify with him before Congress, died, that same day, under equally mysterious circumstances. A few weeks ago, he said to me, "If you hear of my accidental death, don't believe it. It will have been murder." The evidence which could prove that prophecy true or untrue has disappeared from the public domain. Perhaps anticipating this, he hid his documents. No government agency, including the FBI, could find them. They have now been found and are printed here for all of America, for all the world, to see.

Ellen Pettigrew's telephone number was listed on her department's website. Alice Turnbell's phone had a dial tone.

"Hello."

"Professor Pettigrew, this is Tobias Starkey."

"I was so pleased to be told you were alive. I guess the newspapers don't always get it right."

"From where I'm sitting, ma'am, they got it exactly right."

"I assume that means you are happy that people think you don't exist. Even though I would love to know why, I won't ask. Bryce wouldn't say what all the circumstances were. He only said you would call, and you might need me to help out with something. I'm happy to help, however I can."

"Thank you. That's kind of you. I'm working on the death of our friend, John Hamilton." I owed her that much.

"Good for you. I was wondering about that. It didn't add up to me. What can I do?"

"In Hudson, Massachusetts there's a Catholic church, Saint Michael's Parish. There is a woman named Sister Maria who is the keeper of records for the church and their cemetery, which is huge. People buy plots in the cemetery so they have a place to go when they die."

"Yes, I'm aware of that process."

"I need to know who purchased the burial space in Lot 'L', plot 22. Do you think you could find that out for me? I would really appreciate it, Professor, if you could do that."

"I certainly can try. Who is buried there?"

I hesitated, then realized that for her to make up a convincing story, she would have to know that. "The stone says, M.S. Lynxe," I spelled it out. Born, 1992, died, 2016. Then it says, *Vox in Clamantis Deserto.*"

"Oh, dear. Is that Mary Sue Lynxe?"

"You remember her?"

"Vividly. Do you think it is her?"

"It would seem so."

"Oh, dear me. Okay. Being a Dartmouth professor may help. Just musing a bit here, but perhaps I think the College might owe her family a refund of some sort, but we can't find them. Something like that. I'll get on it right now. It's quiet here, I have time and it's only about an hour's drive. Who purchased the burial plot, 'L-22'? Is that right?"

"Yes, that's all I need."

"When I find the name, how shall I get it to you?"

I looked at the phone set. There was an answering system on it. There were no waiting messages. No blinking light.

"Call this phone." I gave her the number. "If I don't answer, leave a message with just the name, and please, no, 'Hello, Tobias', or anything like that, if you could, just the name. I don't want there to be a record of me being where I am right now. Is that okay with you?"

"Yes. Is there anything else I should know?"

Did she need to know that John Hamilton's grave was fifty feet away? "No, nothing I can think of, and thank you so much."

"I'll be at home all Christmas vacation if there's anything else you need. Stay safe, Tobias. I'll call soon."

* * *

I needed clean clothes and a cold beer. The Coop was open. I bought underpants, socks, tee shirts, blue jeans, a pair of slacks, a dark grey, zip-up jacket and a matching grey cap. Everything had the Harvard logo on it, even the underpants. Wearing all this might make it easier to go in and out of Dr. Turnbell's office without raising suspicion. I needed money. I paid for my clothes with Bryce's Visa card and used his ATM to withdraw cash. A few blocks away on Mt. Auburn Street there a was a bar, down some concrete steps underneath an old brick building. It bustled with the chatter and laughter of local people. They didn't all look like students or teachers. Most looked like plumbers and electricians. Perfect. I kept the jacket and the hat in the bag and ordered a pint of Sam Adams and a hamburger.

The bar clock said ten past ten. I was sitting next to a petite blonde girl. She was talking to a plump fellow with a Red Sox hat, about computer hacking, how she was able to find things out from government records without them knowing. The guy said, "All you MIT girls know how to do this?"

"No, they don't teach us that, but after a couple of years of computer science, it's easy to figure out. Just don't obey any rules. That's the trick." It was pretty clear they didn't know each other. She was alone and probably a local student living at home. Not away on Christmas vacation—out for a drink.

What did I need? What could this MIT bit of a thing find out for me that I could never find out myself? The barkeep came by and the girl asked for another drink. She put two crumpled one dollar bills on the counter and was counting quarters from her change purse to make up the balance. I told the barman it would be on me. She gave me a funny look and I asked, "For a hundred dollars, could you find out something for me?"

She turned to face me. "Maybe I would, maybe I wouldn't. Maybe I can, maybe I can't. What is it?"

"I have the license plate number of a British car. A fancy Mercedes Benz. I need to find out who owns it and where they live…Interested?"

"Yeah. Go on. More?"

"It is a very wealthy man who lives in a mansion by the ocean. He has a swimming pool in the back yard facing the sea. Across the road by the shore is a very tall, old stone tower with narrow windows. That's all I know. What do you think?"

She took out her smart phone and googled something up, scrolled down, read something, scrolled again and then said, "Yes, I can do that."

"What did you find out?"

"That British license plates are lettered and numbered in such a way that they identify the area within an eighty kilometer or so radius of where the registration took place, and when. There can't be many mansions with swimming pools across the street from old stone towers in whatever area that is. So, yeah, for two hundred bucks, not one, I'll find out where they live and what their name is. You on?"

"How about in that other hundred you find out everything you can about this person? Who he is, where he comes from and what he does."

"It's a 'he'?"

"Yeah, pretty sure."

"Okay. Can't promise anything, but I'll hack my little heart out."

"How soon. I've got a time problem."

"Noon tomorrow, here."

"A hundred now, a hundred tomorrow, okay?"

She nodded. I gave her five twenties. I took my notes out of my wallet and found the number of the license plate … AV16 PBR.

A burly plumber took issue with an equally burly electrician. They were arguing, shouting at each other about Trump. The plumber thought he was the savior of working people and the electrician thought we was a dangerous Fascist and a 'fucking moron.' A beer bottle spilled. It was getting loud and tense. The bartender was telling them to knock it off or get out. I opened my Coop bag, put on my Harvard cap and walked back to Dr. Turnbell's office.

The red light on the answering machine was blinking. I pushed the button. *You have one new message.* Then Ellen Pettigrew's voice.

'Sarah Bingham.'

Sarah Bingham.

Sarah Bingham. My mother.

I made the sofa into a bed, fumbled my way down the hallway until I found a bathroom, gargled, splashed water on my face, went back to the office, deleted the message and crawled onto the sofa.

20

SARAH BINGHAM, MY MOTHER'S MAIDEN NAME. Who would know that? Without a hunch and some serious research, nobody. He had asked her to do him a favor. Something neither he nor his wife, Jane, could do without leaving a trail. Probably told her at least a part of what it was all about, but not everything. Not enough so she would have said no. Then suggested it would be a great time for her to take her sabbatical. Her son was going to have to do something difficult, possibly dangerous. Her presence would make it more difficult, more dangerous. That's why she didn't cry when she left me. She wasn't leaving her child, she was saying good-bye to a grown man, a man about the same age her husband had been when he went off to war.

I folded up the sheet and blanket as best I could, put them in a pile on the end of the sofa, and pulled the curtain on the window. Harvard Square was just beginning to rustle. People with coffee walking slowly, thoughtfully, saying good morning to each other. It was too early to hurry. The whole day lay ahead. My car, no, my mother's car, was in Hanover. Just as well, it should stay there until all this was over.

Expedia.com listed two rental car places within walking distance. Budget sounded good. My new clothes fit. The jacket looked snappy with its *Veritas* logo. It was all about that, wasn't it—*Veritas*. 'Truth'.

That motto beat the hell out of Dartmouth's convoluted saying. At least people knew what it meant, even if half the population pretended it didn't exist. They knew. I had to believe that.

I had all day to write. There was no need to rent the car and drive to Hudson until dusk. The weather report projected light snow tonight. That should mean it would be dark and hard to see. That was good.

I decided to write three pieces. The headline would, of course, be whatever explosive evidence emerged from the files. That I couldn't write yet. The second would be the story I had started about the mystery surrounding John Hamilton's death. Even if murder could not be conclusive, it would certainly put an exclamation point on the story. The third part, a fact by fact summary of the hunt for the truth about his death and the hunt for the files starting with that day my mother brought me down the road to his house, winding through the connection between Beanie Weeks and Mary Sue Lynxe, the graveyard, the avalanche to the day the files were found would justify publication for the world to see.

The main reason for a newspaper to print that third part would be to demonstrate to the public that this was not fake news, that journalism was not a matter of inventing things and back-proving them later. It was a methodical, ethical process of unearthing the facts and presenting them to the people. Likely they would not want to publish that part. They would want to keep it close to the vest until the government filed defamation and libel charges alleging the story was negligently and willfully fabricated to defame the President of the United States. Then, in an emergency hearing, they would show it to the court, and, almost certainly, the court would vindicate the *Globe,* approve publication, blast the government and everybody would duck for cover.

That piece could not betray any confidences that might cause pain and suffering. Sources, like Alice Turnbell, Benjoin Guimond or Beanie Weeks would remain confidential. But it had to be real and had to be ready to go at the same time as the other two. I would hand all three to Borstien and let the editors cut them up, rearrange them, work them over to meet a print deadline and scoop everybody else. Maybe 3 pm tomorrow or the day after.

There was that piece of information I didn't, and wouldn't, have until noon. Mr. Hamilton had said, 'find the Israeli.' The hacker was on it.

I finished the story of John Hamilton's death. It certainly couldn't be proven he was murdered, not without an autopsy and ballistics report, but all signs pointed that way. I knew it should be no more than 1,500 words to fit as a lead story. Near on noon, I was done. 2,000 words — gave them 500 to cut.

The bar was dark and cool. The hacker girl sat at a booth near the back. She was drinking a cup of coffee.

"What did you find out?"

"Let's take this slow. First, the registration was issued in Ipswich, about an hour north of London. AV16 PBR. 'A' is for Anglia, the region, 'V' is for Ipswich. 16 is the year of first registration of this car. It is a Mercedes Benz S-650 and gets into your garage for about 200 grand. The PBR is random letters that don't mean anything. The car is registered to a Ben Hamilton-Baille, a fine British name that doesn't appear anywhere in any other records.

"Okay, Goggle Map. All along the coast within 40 miles, there is only one stone castle. The Prine Column. Good so far. Near there, there is, once again, only one house that has both a view of the tower and a swimming pool. Address is: 44 Blankenship Rd. IP 41, Kennetville, Ipswich. That's the house."

She had this all on her computer, no paper. I had to make my own notes because I didn't want it sent to Turnbell's computer. Too risky.

"Okay, who is he?"

"Depends on who wants to know?"

"Ah, you don't need my name."

"That's not what I meant. He's got at least three names, probably more, depending upon which country he's in."

"Alright, who does it look like he really is? How about that?'

"The house is owned by Mohan Mizachi. Israeli. The car is registered to Hamilton-Baille, British." She spelled them out. "Tax and business records show him to both a British and Israeli citizen and to own a Mercedes Benz S-650. Birthplace — London. His principal business is listed as MM Model Management and his principal place of business is Haifa, Israel." She sat, quiet, sipping her coffee, looking at me as though I'd done something wrong. Her head tipped to the side, forehead wrinkled, mouth set hard.

"Israeli records are very hard to get into, but it looked to me like this modeling agency was more like an international escort company with branch offices in twelve different cities. You know, like escorts in Beijing, Moscow, Paris, Damascus, like that. Hard to tell, though.

"This is a picture of him from his British driver's license." She turned her computer around. It was absolutely the white-haired man in the motel videos. She waited, sipping, thinking.

"So, that's not all?" I asked.

"No, it isn't. That isn't who he is. There is no birth record in England of anybody named Mohan Mizachi. But that name did turn up in a memorial service article I found for a man named Richard

Jimson. It was from the English language edition of *The Moscow Times*. This Jimson guy was meeting with the most senior Russian Military Intelligence Officers and died of a heart attack in Moscow. For some reason it seemed to be nearly a State funeral. The article mentioned that a Mohan Mizachi was an honored guest.

"Look at this picture. It's of the service. The article says the Mizachi guy is a friend of Mr. Jimson. But look here at the photo. See him?" She handed me a magnifying glass.

"That's him, alright. No doubt."

"And," she said, "read the caption under the photo."

The photo was of six somber people, shoulder to shoulder. It listed the six people, one of whom, and identified by location, was *Richard Jimson Jr., son of the deceased.* Another name, one that I recognized, was Alexander Dugin, a renowned Russian fascist close to the GRU and Putin.

I realized that the people who write the articles get their information from the State, but photographer's get the names by asking the people who they are. That they didn't match was an editorial oversight.

"The real funeral was in Birmingham in 2015. The old man was 92. He was, it said, survived by his son, Richard Jimson Jr. It said the boy was "cut from the same fine Southern cloth.""

"So, Okay. Is that Jimson, like the flower?"

"It's not a flower, it's a weed. Jimsonweed. Poisonous. Noxious. These are very bad people. Scary bad. Richard Jimson Sr. was a white supremacist born in Birmingham, Alabama. An American Fascist. A close advisor to, early on, George Wallace and, later, KKK guy David Duke and Neo-Nazi Richard Spencer. Your guy is his son, born in Tupelo, Mississippi, 1949. His mother, Anna Friesh, interestingly, a Jewess, died in a car wreck when he was two. Ergo, Israeli citizen.

This Jimson Jr. is an international imposter hooked up with Putin. After looking at a few of the other modeling agencies, I'm thinking his escort service may be an international espionage ring. They only deal with high-ranking government officials, like French, German, American, Chinese, like that.

"Oh, and also, he's not an American anymore. You won't find him in that data base. He renounced his citizenship the day Barack Obama was elected."

She put her elbows on the table, wove her fingers together and put her chin on her thumbs.

"I want out of this, now. I don't want to have anything to do with these people. They are fascists. I feel stained, almost abused. I want an extra hundred bucks. It took me all night and I'm done. No more questions. I don't know your name and I don't want to know your name. And to you, I don't have a name, I don't look like anything and I was never here. I'm going to scrub my hard drive and dump it all."

I gave her the money and she left. What was Trump doing hooked up with American Neo-Nazis and Putin's people? Espionage hookers? I suppose that given the situation in America now it wasn't all that far-fetched. Terrifying and so terribly sad, but not so improbable. Back in Turnbell's office, I locked the door and went to work.

I wrote all day. By afternoon, the second and third parts were done. The third part included watching Jim Lacey fire his pistol, aimed at me, triggering an avalanche and the purposeful and duplicitous construction of my supposed death. Writing this had been hard, like taking Truman Capote's *In Cold Blood* and turning the whole thing into a few five page vignettes. Both pieces were still too long to fit in a newspaper article, but that was not my problem. That was for Borstien and his people to fix. Give them everything and let them decide what was important. It occurred to me that I was going to have to cut a deal with Borstien — I get to approve the final print edition and my name goes on it. Maybe that was normal. Probably not. I'll ask Jasmine on my way into the corner office.

My mind began playing tricks on me. I was trying to convince myself that I could get these files out of the grave without Maggie. Somebody had to stand guard, to alert me of danger that I wouldn't hear or see because I was in a hole clawing at a casket. I needed her, one voice said. Don't risk it, another answered back. This was the most dangerous part of the whole journey. If something were to happen to her, Daddy would pull stings to get us out of serious trouble, then he would have his boys beat me to a pulp and throw me in a dumpster. But all she had to do was stand, look and listen. She wouldn't be part of it. She'd be safe. This went on, back and forth until my mind lost and my heart won. I picked up the phone and called the Hall of Records.

"Hall of Records, this is Tania."

"Good afternoon, Tania, I'm calling for Senator Bonwit. Is your director, Ms. James in? The Senator has a question for her." That ought to get her to the phone. I tried to make my voice low, so Tania wouldn't recognize it.

"Hello. This is Maggie James; how can I help you?"

"Do not make a peep. Don't squeal. Don't say anything. Look straight ahead. Don't say my name. I am not dead. I am fine, but I need to kiss you and then ask you to help me. Today, tonight. Can you?"

There was deep, labored breathing, then, "Yes. Where? When?"

"Harvard Square. Bench by the T-stop. One hour."

"I think I love you."

"The Senator prefers more direct statements."

"I love you."

"I love you, too. Wear dark clothing."

Budget had the car I wanted. Small, cheap and black. I put it on Bryce's credit card. The government guys had no reason to track him. They knew where he was—in Hanover. A few blocks away was a hardware store. I bought a short-handled, flat-bladed shovel, a hammer, a pry bar, a bag of red mechanic's cloths, a small box of black plastic trash bags and a pot of Christmas poinsettias, just in case we had to, all of a sudden, be doing nothing more than leaving flowers at a loved one's tombstone. I put them in the trunk and parked in a garage on Eliot Street, a few blocks from the Square. A light snow was beginning to fall.

Maggie launched herself at me from five feet away. I almost fell over backwards. She wrapped her legs around me and like she always did, buried her face in my neck. She writhed and giggled and gave me a hickey. It was more than a public display of affection. It was almost illegal.

"I've only been dead a couple of days. Not that bad."

"What happened?"

"I'll tell you in the car."

"Where are we going?"

"To Hudson. About thirty miles west of here."

"And?"

"We're going to rob a grave."

She stopped all her wiggling and squeaking. She stood still, back straight, shoulders square. "You have to be kidding."

"I'm not."

"Oh boy, oh boy, oh boy, my daddy's going to be really proud of his little girl this time. She stole a dead body right out of the ground in the middle of the night. That is not just a youthful prank, Tobias."

"I hope he will be proud, otherwise he will kill me and I will actually be dead. There isn't a body in the grave."

"You found the files, didn't you?"

"I think so. Yeah, I'm almost positive. Let's go, it's getting dark."

We walked, shoulder to shoulder, hand in hand down the street and into the parking garage. Maggie's mind was not fixed on the task ahead. She kept asking if she could sleep with me on the teacher's sofa. I sensed she thought there was something tantalizingly naughty in that idea. I tried my best to lay out what we had to do—where everything was, who was going to do what and how much time we would have. She wanted to know if the sofa was leather or upholstery.

Maggie *had* been paying attention. When we got to the hill above the cemetery, she pointed to a paved area behind the convenience store where a few cars were parked. "Employee parking," she said. "This is perfect."

I put the tools in a black plastic bag. She carried the poinsettia. We walked together through the entry arch and made our way along the roads to section 'L' and up to plot #16. Maggie knelt at John Hamilton's grave site, holding the potted flowers. My stomach was churning. I stood in front of May Sue Lynxe's grey tombstone. For some reason, I crossed myself and whispered a prayer.

I shoveled the snow off first, swinging it to the roadside of the grave so it would be a barrier, shielding the dirt from view. The ground was frozen, rock hard. I wrapped a cloth around the curved end of the pry bar to deaden the sound and began hammering the earth to loosen it in chunks. It wasn't frozen deep, just a few inches. The clods came out easily, each the size of a dinner plate. I stacked them in order on the forest side of the grave. I began to shovel, throwing the dirt beyond the clods. It became a large pile of rich, black earth, but, only two feet down, I hit something solid. Solid and hollow.

Maggie whispered, loud enough for me to hear, "Stop shoveling, get down."

I could see headlights of a car slowing down near the entrance. Hunched over, kneeling, I watched. It felt like it was too dark, and we were too far away, for them to see us. The car didn't stop, it drove past the entry, around a curve and out of sight.

I shoveled faster. It was a wooden box, about six feet long, the size of a coffin. I latched my fingers on an edge and pulled. It didn't budge. It was nailed shut. I took the pry bar and tapped it in below the lip and pushed. The lid moved. I slid it along the wedged opening, prying up. It made a squeal every time I pushed.

"Shhh!" Maggie whispered. "Keep it down."

Headlights would occasionally pass by the cemetery, but the only ones that swung across the graves were cars pulling out of the store. The driver's eyes would be on the road, making the turn.

The last squeal was a loud one, but the lid came free. It hadn't taken long. It wasn't as hard to pry loose as I had expected. I tossed it to the side.

"Oh my God! Oh, no! Shit!"

"What?" Maggie's whisper was urgent.

In the coffin, was a brown ceramic urn. An urn for ashes of a cremated person.

"Oh, fuck, Tobias, we got to get out of here. There's a person in that grave." She tapped me on the back. "We got to leave, now!"

"Maggie, come here." She put the flowers down and came up beside me. She bent over and I picked the urn out of the casket and put it in her hands. "I'll put everything back, then we go."

"Are you crazy, Tobias? This might be a dead person in here."

I threw the rags and tools into the coffin, dropped the lid on it, shoveled the dirt back on, placed the clods on top and shoveled snow on the lumpy mound. I put the shovel in the plastic bag, slung it over my shoulder, tugged Maggie's sleeve, and walked fast down the road.

In the car, she calmed down, collected herself, adjusting her head, neck, shoulders and back. She held the urn between her legs. She smiled over at me.

"Sorry I got a little freaked out. Probably a little normal for first-time grave robber, but I'm feeling much better now. Something just occurred to me. Tobias, was that lid hard to get off?"

"No, it came off easy. Why?"

She lifted the urn. "Coffin lids are nailed the fuck shut with lots of big nails. Keep the creepy-crawly things out for a while. Give the newly departed a few weeks of peace and quiet before the ants and beetles gnaw their way in. This urn, I'm starting to think it's just like the toaster."

We parked the car in a twenty-four-hour garage and walked the empty streets back to Boylston Hall. Harvard Square was quiet, settled into the night. The Campus Police night watchman waved a short wave as we entered through the gate off Mass. Ave. He seemed to know who I was, or at least that I was allowed to be there.

We spread the trash bag out on Alice Turnbell's office desk and sprinkled the ashes out — carefully, slowly, peering at every little bit that fell into the pile. It smelled like wood smoke, like ashes from a fireplace, not like the burnt remains of an animal. On the last pour, I tapped the bottom of the jug and a USB flash drive, wrapped and taped in a plastic baggie, fell onto the top of the pile. I was exhausted, body and mind. My hands trembled. We hugged and I could feel a shiver in her body. She, as well, was done, spent.

"Tomorrow," I said. "Crack of dawn. It' late. We need to sleep."

"The sofa's leather. I like that."

21

MAGGIE STRUGGLED OFF THE SOFA in the morning.

"Maggie, my dear, you look bedfaced."

"I feel bedfaced. Somehow my head got wedged between the sofa cushion and the arm. Is there a bathroom around here?"

"Down the hall." I handed her Bryce's first aid kit. "There's a comb and toothbrush in there."

Cleaned up, she looked okay. Still a few red splotches on her forehead and cheeks. It made her look a little flushed, but she was so pretty it didn't matter.

She was going to take the T back to Boston, get changed, go to work, and wait for me to call her. She promised she wouldn't say a word to anybody. I told her I wouldn't call until the story had gone to the presses. I didn't know how long it would take.

This much was true. If Maggie hadn't been with me at the graveyard, I would not have dared, no matter that night had fallen, I would not have dared to dig up a grave out in the open. The risk would have been far too great. If she hadn't been there, this flash drive would not be in my pocket. Without her and her daddy, I never would have gotten the documents about Mr. Hamilton's death. If she hadn't handed me the recorder at the Presidential Inn, all set to go, I would never have recorded Jim Lacey. Had none of those things happened, I would not be here, in this office, with a computer, a story and John Hamilton's files. I would have failed. Sure, she blinked at the grave—who wouldn't? But she knew what to do and she knew what not to do—don't chicken out, don't run away—do what you have to do and damn the consequences. Maggie and John Hamilton were a lot alike. I turned on the computer and put in the drive.

The flash drive was what I thought it was going to be. Dozens of pages of notes scanned to the drive. I scrolled through them. Handwritten notes, government documents, passport applications, foreign agent reports, and then, pages and pages of financial documents tracing money through multiple banks, some in the U.S., some overseas. I didn't understand any of it. And then an audio-visual recording.

The first three frames were the same ones I had seen in the Sir John Motel—Ukraine, England and Russia. No audio. This computer had a pause icon and a zoom control. I didn't learn anything new. Mr. Hamilton had said to find out who the white-haired man was. Richard Jimson Jr., white supremacist from Birmingham Alabama. Mr. Hamilton would have known his name and could have found out who he was and what he did if he had been a twenty-year old MIT hacker who didn't care what the laws were, or give a damn about international counter-intelligence protocol agreements.

The next frame was of a wide, busy street in Moscow. The skyline was dotted with the iconic onion domes and star-topped steeples. Once again, no sound. A limousine pulled up to the curb in front of a large, opulent hotel. The lights around the entry were on. The camera was jerky, like it was pinned to a person or a smart phone poking out of a pocket. It zoomed in on an emblem beside the entry door. The logo was distinctive. I paused and googled-up 'logo—lion's head on top of a cross.' Ritz-Carlton Hotels. A couple of burly guys got out. One stood by the front bumper, eyes scanning the people in front of the hotel. The other opened the rear door and Donald Trump got out, smiling. He started into the hotel, then hesitated, waiting for one of the bodyguards to get in front of him.

Another car pulled under the port-cochere, not a limo, but fancy and black. A woman got out alone. A classy woman dressed in a black dress with a plunging neckline and shoulder-length wavy brown hair. I had seen that woman before. I paused and zoomed in. I was sure of it. It was the woman from the Sir John Motel. She stopped on the sidewalk and looked directly at the camera lens. I thought I saw her wink. I zoomed again. Paused, back, back, forward, paused, and there it was. Her left eye was closed. She knew the person with the camera. Was she saying everything is under control? All systems go? She waited while a porter took her bags from the car, then followed Trump into the hotel.

The images inside were still jumpy, but better. The Trump entourage was waived through. One bodyguard stayed behind to accompany the bellhops with the luggage. The three: Trump, the woman and the other bodyguard, who looked like Keith Schiller, Trump's long-time protection guy, waited at the elevator. They got in and went up. The person with the camera waited for a bit, then pushed the button and focused the camera on the floor indicator. The door opened and two men in suits got out. Both had corded earphones, one carried some sort of wand. Had Russian Intelligence swept the room for bugs, then let Trump in? Or had they planted one?

The next frames were in high resolution. A different camera, inside a hotel bedroom. It was a lavish room with doors leading out either side. It was part of a suite. The bed looked big enough for four people. A time and date were displayed at the bottom — 7:07:32 pm — Nov 8 — 2013 —UTC+3.00. Donald Trump was sitting on the edge of the bed, looking at photographs of women in swimsuits. He'd look at one, flip it over and set it on the bed in one of two piles. On the back of each page was written, in English and Russian (I assume the Russian said the same thing)., Miss Universe Contest — November 9, 2013 — and a name and country of that contestant. He had changed his shirt and tie. His hair was combed. It looked like he'd showered before the camera was on. He was humming to himself, sorting the photos in piles. Every two or three pages, he'd clean his hands from a pump top squirter, like a hand-sanitizer. A knock on the door. Trump said "Come in."

Keith Schiller came in and said, "The girls are here, Mr. Trump."

"How many?"

"Two."

"Are they Russians?"

"Yes, one is from Odessa in the Ukraine, but she lives here in Moscow. The other is from Omsk in Siberia. They are both very beautiful, sir."

"Good, give me ten minutes, then send them in."

Schiller left.

Trump turned to someone who was not in the picture and said, "Hey, Pussycat, come back at about midnight. Treat yourself to the town." He tossed a wad of money on the bed. I assumed it was the woman from the Sir John, who seemed to be his mistress for this trip. It was. She came out of the bathroom and picked up the money. It was her. She bussed him on the cheek and left. He continued sorting through his swimsuit pictures.

Schiller held the door open and two women entered. The first to enter was a tall woman wearing a fur hat and a black, thigh-length leather coat. I paused and zoomed in, then scrolled all the way back to the first video of the man in Kiev. This was the woman he had been talking to in the square. Tall, stunning, Slavic blonde. The second woman was a brunette. She was shorter, but no less beautiful. Her facial features were almost Asian.

Trump got off the bed, put his papers in a pile on the desk, and stood, his back to the camera. The lens must have been on the headboard of the bed.

Schiller left.

The tall woman appeared to be helping Trump undo his tie and unbutton his shirt. Trump untied the sash on her coat, spread it open and began running his hands over the curves of her body. The women undressed completely. The taller one put her calf-length boots and fur hat back on.

The next ten minutes were pure pornographic sex. I had never seen anything even close to this. Instead of being aroused, I was nauseated. The women spoke in Russian. Trump only groaned, grunted and swore.

At one point, the taller woman from the first video seemed to adjust her fur hat, then slap his backside. Or did she take something out of the inner band of the hat and jab him with it? It wasn't clear. It seemed more like a jab than a slap, but I couldn't tell. The other woman's arm and leg partially obscured it. I paused, ran back and played in slow-motion. It still wasn't clear. I couldn't see anything in her hand, but that didn't mean there wasn't anything there.

When Trump rolled over, exhausted, large and pink, both women collected their clothing and went into the bathroom together. Water could be heard running. They came out and got dressed. While Trump lay on his side, the shorter one gathered his clothes, folded them and laid them neatly on the bed. The tall one used a cell phone to call someone. They both left. Trump went into bathroom. Again, water could be heard.

A few minutes later, there was a soft knock at the door. Trump was dressed again, cleaning his hands.

"Come in." Four men came in. One was the banker with the goatee and bow tie. He was carrying a briefcase. The other was the white-haired man, the Israeli, from all three of the first videos. The third was the military man who had been at the barbershop in Moscow. The fourth guy was the short, bald one. He had a narrow face and deep-set dark eyes. They were all speaking in Russian.

The Israeli locked the door, then pulled three chairs up close to the bed. The banker opened his briefcase and took out a sheaf of papers. The Israeli walked around the room. He looked like he was talking to himself. The military guy stood at stiff attention. Unmoving, unblinking. The bald guy sat down. Jimson, still walking, spoke.

"Mr. Trump. It is a pleasure to have you here in Moscow. A few months ago, I was asked to coordinate, with these three gentlemen, a top-level briefing for you on your arrival here. That request came from President Putin. We have all agreed on the most important information you should have at your disposal. Please listen carefully. It is vital." He extended his hand out toward the banker.

"Mr. Trump, I am Dimitri Parnov, CEO of Sherbank, the largest bank in Russia. I have spoken with President Putin about our discussion here. He personally granted me privilege to discuss important financial matters." Jimson was translating. His voice was an Alabama drawl, so each statement took a while. "You have had many profitable dealings with Russia, the Ukraine and many of our common allies. A Mr. Paul Manafort and Mr. Felix Sater have participated with you on these endeavors. Am I correct?"

"I know them. Good men. Smart men."

"Yes, but here is a problem, Mr. Trump. Many of these dealings have been, shall we say, poorly reported to your government. There is some legal exposure on your part. I am here to offer assistance with that matter. Accounting documents can be aligned to satisfy these requirements."

"What are you asking me to do?"

"I will get to that in a moment. You and your people, through your attorney, Mr. Cohen, have been seeking permission to build a 'Trump Tower Moscow'. Correct?"

"Yes. That's right. A beautiful thing. Huge and beautiful. Maybe the biggest Trump Tower in the world."

"Yes. I am aware of that. I am here to tell you that my bank will, with the proper asset collateral, provide full funding, or joint funding with other financial institutions, for that project."

"Spectacular. Perfect. Maybe we work with Deutsche Bank. We might be talking a billion dollars."

"I can see that. Yes, we could do that. But, Mr. Trump, there is a problem."

"What's that?"

"The sanctions your president, Mr. Obama and his Secretary of State, Mrs. Clinton, have illegally imposed on Russia are strangling our resources. Not just the whole national economy, but my bank as well. In order for this cooperative agreement to come to life, the sanctions must be lifted in their entirety. Then we can talk. Should you, as we all certainly hope, choose to run for the presidency of your country, and should you be successful, full funding will be available for 'Trump Tower Moscow' the minute those sanctions are lifted.

And to circle back, all accounting of previous investments will be re-aligned. Do you understand my offer?"

"I do. That is a beautiful offer."

He seemed to be staring down into Donald Trump. He put his sheaf of papers back into his briefcase and left the room. He hadn't looked at a single piece of paper. Jimson nodded to the military man.

"Mr. Trump, I am Sergey Shoygu. Minister of Defense. I am also here at the express request of Vladimir Putin, president of the Russian Federation."

"Good to meet you Mr. Shogun."

"Shoygu. Again, as expressed by Dimitri Parnov, all of us hope you enter your presidential race. That, in our view, would benefit the entire world." Trump smiled and nodded. "It is important we talk now, before any announcement on your part. Mr. Putin advised me that after an announcement, all of your dealings and even conversations become subject to intense scrutiny. We need to talk now. Under your presidency, the United States and Russia could form an alliance joining the two most powerful militaries in the world. With China, three. That is possible. Shake their money and their weapons will follow. We could then establish a world order in which regional wars, in the Middle East, in Africa, in the mountains of Afghanistan, could swiftly be resolved and ended. It would, I'm sure you agree, lead to a more peaceful and prosperous world. Others, Turkey, North Korea, and maybe, maybe Israel, could all be brought on board."

Trump was once again smiling, nodding and fingering his long red tie. He started to say something but changed his mind. "Go on, please."

"In order to accomplish that, the socialist confederations of NATO and the European Union need to be weakened, to be made, how shall I say, impotent. Then a world order based on military and financial strength can be put in place. An order where money is controlled by people who know how to control money and not by people who want to give it all away to the lazy and the poor. Strength, Mr. Trump."

"I couldn't agree more."

"Thank you. You are a very smart man. I'm sure we can work together." He snapped back to military attention.

The bald man in the chair spoke next. His English was accented, but good enough to understand. "I am Fydor Mayakovsky, Director of Russian Intelligence.

"Mr. Putin believes, as do many, that if your election were today, or even in the near future, Mrs. Hilary Clinton would win by a large number of votes. We can change that. Again, on the promise of an end to sanctions and political cooperation between our nations as my colleagues have said, we can almost ensure you win the presidency. Are you willing to accept our assistance on those terms?"

"Absolutely. Sanctions are a bad way of governing. Good businessmen lose money."

"Fine. At my disposal is the entire cyber-security capability of the military and the intelligence agencies of the Russian Federation. Your federal government doesn't control your elections, individual states do. It's like shooting ducks in a pond. Pick the one you want and," he put his finger and thumb like a pistol, "boom! you win. Easy. Give us your approval, here, now, and I will unleash these forces in such a way as to conclusively alter the outcome of your election. Surround yourself with people who are loyal to the end. That includes your intelligence directors. Most important. Do not let intelligence dictate policy. You must set your goals and make the intelligence follow. If you don't do that, we can't help you.

"We already have many of your people on board—Mr. McConnell in your Senate, many congressmen and the most powerful lobby in your country, the NRA, they are with us. No sanctions, alliance with Russia, weaken the E.U, weaken NATO. President Donald Trump. Those are the terms. Do you agree?"

"I don't have to think about that for a minute. It's a beautiful idea. Huge. I love it. The answer is yes."

The GRU stood up. The general extended his hand and Trump shook it, still sitting on his bed. They left together. Trump looked a little shell-shocked. He stood and faced Richard Jimson. "Who are you?"

Jimson sat in one of the chairs. Trump sat back down on the bed.

"My name is Richard Jimson, Mr. Trump. I deal in espionage around the world. Much of the information you have heard here today came from my work. I am also here at the request of Mr. Putin. I would not say I am a friend of his. I would say no one is. He asked me to be here. This is, like most things in Russia, his idea. Mr. Trump, do you remember George Wallace?"

"Yes, of course."

"My father was a close confidant of Wallace, and others who believed in a strong, enduring, white America. I also believe in that goal. George Wallace knew something others didn't know. He knew it isn't only the south that believes in the supremacy of the white race, it is all of America. I believe, Mr. Trump, to win and to win again, and again, you must gather all those people to your side. Loyal and strong followers. You need to bring them up, bring them out and light them on fire. There are millions and millions of them. Then you can win."

Trump said nothing.

"I have a piece of advice. You can win in 2016 with help from Putin and if you fire up a base that will follow you. Then, there is one way you will certainly win again and again. One way, Mr. Trump."

"I like this. It's good. What's that way to win and win again?"

"Start a Civil War."

"Huh?"

"Start the Second Civil War. Your people, the defenders of the Second Amendment, going right at the blacks, the Hispanics and the liberal elite. Violently. Presidents don't lose elections during a war. Then, and this is my final comment, end the war. Bring peace to the country. You will be a hero, Mr. Trump, you will be the greatest president the country has ever had. You, Mr. Trump, you." Jimson stood in front of him, waiting for a reply.

Trump sat like a stone staring at his feet, blinking, flicking his red tie, then said, "I got it. You're right."

"And stay the TV Reality guy in front of the camera. Don't change. They love it." Jimson smiled and left. Trump sanitized his hands and went into the bathroom.

There was a break in the video. It stopped at 8:22 pm — Nov 8 — 2013—UTC-+3.00. It resumed about four hours later. I assumed he had left to go preside over the Miss Universe Contest and the room had been empty. At 12:13 am, the door opened and the woman from the Sir John Motel came in. Trump was on the bed, apparently sound asleep in his clothes. She could be seen walking towards the camera. Her hand occupied the entire screen. The screen went black.

22

I NEEDED COFFEE, FOOD AND TIME TO THINK. The flash drive zipped into the inside pocket of my Harvard jacket, I took the bag of ashes and went out into the streets. There I was, walking around Cambridge with international security secrets in my coat.

I was hungry and scared and couldn't risk leaving them in a Harvard faculty office. The file was terrifying. It became clear that I was going to have to go back to the Sir John Motel and find that woman. What was her name? I got my notes out of my wallet. Candi Duvall. A stage name. Who was she really? One of Trump's mistresses? A deep cover agent working for John Hamilton? Both of those? The only way to find out was to ask her. The only way she might answer, was if she knew I had found the files. It occurred to me, that when she showed me the first three frames in that sleazy motel room, she had no idea where Mr. Hamilton was going to hide his files. He never told her. Nobody had known, not even his wife. But Jane Hamilton had said she smelled things burning in the fireplace late at night. That's what the ashes were. They were all his notes and papers, scanned to a flash disc, then wadded up and stuffed into the burning oak and cherry logs. All his files, so sensitive that he wouldn't give them to James Comey, his boss, were on the flash drive in my jacket pocket. So sensitive that he had buried it sometime before he was scheduled to testify to the Secret Select Committee. Somebody made sure he would never talk to them.

If I had any chance of getting all this to the presses before Christmas, I would have to go to the motel this afternoon, with the files on my person. Candi Duvall was the only contact I had who would know how this came about and who had gotten this surveillance tape. I had wiped Turnbell's computer clean. The only record was on my file, in my pocket.

I found the Pink Filly online. The man on the phone said Candi Duvall was there but she was working. She'd be off in half an hour. I asked him to tell her that Tobias Starkey needed to talk to her. He said he would.

Christmas was near. The holiday spirit seemed to have energized men to get out of the office, out of their homes, away from their wives and children, and have their own special time before presents and turkey dinner, reveling in alcohol and naked women in Santa hats gyrating on shiny poles, crawling around on all fours, twerking in their faces and taking their money. The parking lot was nearly full. I was ten minutes early.

I walked around to the front of the motel to see if I could find the Navy Seal. No lights went on. I banged on the door and no answer came. No one was there. Trash had blown up onto the walkway. I went back through the parking lot and in through the from door of the Pink Filly. A bouncer asked for my ID. The place was dark, crowded and smelled of beer. In the center of rings of chairs was a platform and in the middle of that was a tall, shiny pole. A woman, naked but for a few strings, was gyrating around and men were shouting and whistling. The woman finished and walked around the edge of the platform while men stuck money in the strings and between her breasts. The woman was a young African-American. When she had made her final round, the announcer boomed over the loud-speaker, "Gentlemen, a round of applause for the wet and wild Candi Duvall!"

All the way back to Harvard Square, I kept turning over in my mind the mistakes I had made, the things I had overlooked. I should have listened more closely to Dr. Turnbell's story about the bombing mastermind. The smoke and mirrors of it all.

I had been dead for three days. I was completely worn out. I was going to make more mistakes if I wasn't very careful. How many cracks were there in the story of my death? Bryce knew I was alive. How long could he hold up doing something that was absolutely contrary to his fundamental character? How long could he hold a lie inside until he had to unburden to somebody? His mother or father in Strupps Corner, Alabama? A sister? Ellen Pettigrew knew. She would have no reason to tell anyone until the FBI showed up at her office. She didn't know why it was important that I was dead.

So, then, who knows? Maggie was surely twisting and chewing on strands of her hair like she did whenever she got nervous. Sitting in the bar, saying nothing to her Daddy until her Daddy had had enough of vacant stares and hair-chewing and demanded to know just what was eating at her? Alice Turnbell? Who was she beyond the renowned professor? She worked with the FBI. Did she work *for* them as well? There were at least four cracks in the vault that kept me dead, sealed away from, as Jane Hamilton had called them, the rogue agents. I needed sleep. I needed it now.

I jolted in my car seat. The Patriot Act! That law that demanded to know who was traveling where and when—by airplane, train, bus and ferry. Photo identification entered into the mega-data base and speed scanned by monster computers. Bryce Haskell could not have bought a ticket on the Concord Coach from Wildcat Mountain to Boston when he was sitting in Hanover, New Hampshire. That girl....Zoe...reads the paper, she's going to say, *Wow, the guy who raced the avalanche and beat it was here today. I sold him a ticket to Boston. That's cool. Can't wait to tell Bob.* That little piece of information, that tiny entry of just a name, time and place in a spread sheet of thousands and thousands of tiny entries in a massive data base would be flagged red if Bryce's name had been put with mine on any watch list. He rented a car in Cambridge while Tobias Starkey's mother's car sat in the parking lot of #14 Blanchard Square, Hanover. The feds had probably parked right next to it, looking at the license plate when they went in to grill him, as they certainly would have.

The cracks in the vault were too big. They were going to get me. When? Maybe tomorrow. Maybe right now. I sprinted into the Yard. The security man was there. He held up his hand.

"Just thought you ought to know, Dr. Turnbell is in her office."

"Alone?"

"No, three guys came in with her."

"Harvard guys?"

"No, not that I recognize."

"What did they look like? Not that it's any of my business, but maybe I know them. Then it would be okay for me to go up. If not, I probably shouldn't bust in." My hand was gripping my pantleg to keep my knee from shaking.

"Good point. One was real tall and walked with a limp. Another guy had really bushy eyebrows and a kind-of big nose and the third guy was tall and skinny, narrow head. They were all wearing suits."

"No," I said, shaking my head, "they don't ring a bell. I don't think I know them. Better to leave her alone. I'll just go to Grendle's Den and have a beer. Thanks for the head's up."

I turned and walked back out the gate, around the corner beyond a hedgerow and broke into a run. Don't run on the streets. Get off the streets. Get out of sight. I cut across the Square and down the steps deep into the bowels of the MBTA Harvard Square Station. *Holy Shit!*—rogue agents—Lacey, Donovan and Worthy.

It was almost empty. Hard tile, concrete, vaulted ceiling—a tube-like mausoleum for the last living—waiting for a noise, any noise, to echo. A couple, intertwined as one. A man in sweatpants and a giant Celtics jersey watching two schoolgirls with long thin schoolgirl legs in matching striped leggings leaning against a column, surfing their cell phones, oblivious. Two bearded young men cross-legged on the floor with a chessboard between them. They looked like Bolsheviks. A rotund cop walking, waddling away on his beat, then turning back.

I sat on the cold floor by the Bolsheviks, pulled my legs cross-legged, took off my coat and hat, messed up my hair and stared intently at their game. The had a timer clock. TICK—TICK—TICK. Each tick an eternity. They gave me no notice. The cop gave me no notice. He ambled to the entrance, looked up, turned and ambled back on his beat through the tube to its other end. I was going to take the next train to wherever it went, to wherever wasn't here. I was on the inbound side of the tracks. I'm going inbound, but nowhere near the *Globe,* nowhere near Maggie or the Old South Ender.

A minute later, the train roared into the station pushing a cone of cold air. The Celtic jersey fluttered and the wheels, desperately in need of oil, screamed as it braked to a stop. The few there who were going somewhere lined up at the edge of the gap. The Bolsheviks didn't budge or even look up. The doors opened and I was in. The doors closed and I was safe. Only a handful of people were in my car—mostly students and an old man with a worn-out satchel clutched between his knees. He stared down at the floor, not even caring who came or went. I sensed he had ridden this train, at this time, going to that place, hundreds of times before.

The voice in the box called out: Central, then Kendall, Charles, Park, Downtown Crossing. The whole thing banged and jostled like a bad carnival ride. I was tempted to jump out into the maw where the most people might be, but I stayed in my seat. The *Globe* was too close nearby. Next stop, South Station and I bolted through the doors and into the clutch of busses and trains and cabs. The station wasn't full, but it wasn't empty either. People were going places in the middle of the night. An old, ornate clock high on a stone arch leading to the big trains said 12:45. There must have been more than a dozen platforms, some empty, some with trains waiting to go someplace far away.

I went to a kiosk and searched the schedules. There was my train—Washington, D.C.—leaving platform #6 at 12:55. A red-eye arriving at Union Station at 8:10 AM. Perfect. This train was leaving in ten minutes. I paid him cash.

I grabbed the ticket and ran down the wide colonnade to platform #6. The whistle was blowing and I slid through the door as the conductor shouted, "Last Call! All Aboard! Acela Line—New York City, Philadelphia, Baltimore, Washington D.C.—All Aboard!"

The ticket lady came. She wore a snappy blue outfit with a round, flat-billed hat. I gave her my ticket and asked if I could sleep all the way through to Washington.

"Sure," she said, "if you can sleep through Penn Station, you get an award. I'll wake you up when we get near Washington." I put my hand in my pocket to feel the file, took my credit card and driver's license out, took my shoe off, and slid them into my sock, then, finally, all used up, fell sound asleep.

23

THE TICKET LADY SHOOK ME AWAKE. Her uniform was not so snappy as it was eight hours ago. It was wrinkled, like she had taken a few naps herself. There seemed to be some creases of worry on her face.

"Here's your award, honey. We're about ten minutes from Union Station." She handed me two chocolate mint patties and a handi-wipe. "We're about two hours late. You slept through all the commotion. It's almost 10:30. Held up in Baltimore. Somebody jammed the track switch. All kinds of problems. You be careful out there. You haven't heard the announcements the conductor has been making, so I'll tell you—there are a lot, I mean a lot of very angry people out on those streets. Angry and violent. Lots of them."

"Oh yeah? How come? What happened?"

"Lord only knows, but it's best to take a cab and get out of downtown." She patted my shoulder. "Watch out for yourself." She moved on down the aisle. The train car was now packed, every seat.

I hadn't heard any news for five days. I looked out the window as we approached the station and there were, just as she said, a whole lot of people out on the streets. Not quite shoulder to shoulder, but pretty close. Where'd they all come from? There were a lot of MAGA hats and American flags. I looked up the aisle and people were getting ready to get off, pulling their baggage with them.

In the back of the car was a group of young people with signs that said, 'Stop Fascism Now!' A fight broke out in the aisle. Pushing, shouting. The ticket lady, tough as nails, barged her way into the middle of the fracas, dragged them apart, pointed her fingers in the faces of both groups and growled, "Y'all want to fight, that's fine, but don't fight on my train. G'won out in the streets and fight like you came here to do. Ain't no TV cameras on this train. Now cut it out!" She looked exhausted.

After the train hissed its last hiss, the doors opened and I went out into the station, jostled about by my fellow trainmates and, more pushed than walked, out onto the street. I could see the dome of the Capitol six or eight blocks away. Between me and the dome, it was solid people. No way to walk there. It was not going to be possible to saunter into the U.S. Capitol and find a senator to talk to. I turned to a big man beside me. He was barrel-chested with a full white beard, a black POW bandana and a black leather jacket.

"Excuse me sir, why are all these people here. What's going on?"

"You born yesterday, boy? We come here to take back our government. Take it back for the people." He pointed to the dome. "We're gonna kill them fuckin' Muslim Communists." He swung his jacket open and there was a pistol shoved into his waistband. "All of 'em. Every last fuckin' one of them. We are Homeland Security. You're lookin' at it."

I bolted. I ran back away from the crowds. The stores were all boarded up. Nothing was open.

I had no idea where the *Washington Post* was in this town and I was certain that if I asked one of those people out there, they would shoot me. I pulled out my steno pad. No senator, no newspaper, Plan 'C'. J. William Conklin. Attorney at Law. Flipping through the steno pages, there it was—Conklin Kennedy – 1st and D. The crowds were still a few blocks away. There was a man ahead locking a door. My pace quickened and I got to him as he was opening a car door. He did not want to talk, but my question was simple—where is 1st and D? He pointed down the street and jerked his thumb to the left, closed his car door and drove off. I could hear gunfire.

Ten minutes later, I was standing in front of a massive wooden door with a large brass handle. It was set in an alcove. The sign beside the door said, *Conklin Kennedy LLP*. The door was locked. If there was a talk box, it was too well hidden. The gunfire was nearer, louder, more. Sirens started. I banged on the door and shouted, "Mr. Conklin! Mr. Conklin! Are you there? Hello, Mr. Conklin!". I backed out on the street and looked up at the building. Two stories above, a window cranked open and a woman's head poked out.

"Yes, can I help you?"

"Yes, please. My name is Tobias Starkey. I am a journalist from Boston. I met Mr. Conklin at an inn in Pequot Falls, NH. He said to come here if I really needed help. I really need help, right now. I have to talk to him. It is very important."

"What is this concerning?"

I stepped back, breathed deeply, looked up and said, "It concerns why Vladimir Putin created this riot."

Long seconds passed. A buzzer sounded at the door. I pushed the great brass handle and it swung open, smooth and easy. She was standing at the top of a wide, curving staircase. She beckoned me up.

The great one, the lion of civil rights, defender of the First Amendment, sat in a leather chair in a room set up like a living room. The windows looked out on the U.S. Capitol and the Supreme Court building beyond. Other plush chairs surrounded a polished coffee table. The only thing on the table was a telephone.

"Well, my young friend, it's good to see you again. Might I deduce that you have found something in your search that requires my immediate attention? Mind you, we were all about to vacate these premises before we get eviscerated by lawless, vicious criminals."

"No, sir. What I have does not require your attention. It requires the attention of the Senate Select Intelligence Committee and the *Washington Post*. I am here to ask you to help me get in touch with them right now, not this afternoon, not tonight, but right now. I almost got shot just walking around out there. I wouldn't make it on my own. I need your help." I held up the flash drive file. "I found John Hamilton's file. He had buried it in an empty grave. It is a video of Donald Trump being indoctrinated by Vladimir Putin in a hotel in Moscow. It is why this riot is happening. It was planned years ago."

"Abigail, bring me my laptop. I assume you will let me verify these allegations to my satisfaction before calling in all my political chits. Am I right?

"Yes, sir." I didn't want to do it this way, but I had no choice.

He slid the drive into his computer, turned the sound up and began watching. It started with three frames of the Israeli. He bent his head to the screen and occasionally grunted. When it got to all the documents, I suggested he skip ahead. He did, mumbling something about "discovery phase." It came to the Ritz Carlton Moscow. He clearly recognized it. As he watched and listened to the Audio-Visual tape, his face became reddened. His eyes squinted, he leaned in closer and his mouth began opening and closing, like a fish. The banker, the Minister of Defense, and then he burst out.

"That miserable snake. Jimson! A fugus on our fine society! My Good Lord, are we witnessing the second Battle of Bull Run? Is that what is happening outside these windows? Mr. Starkey, how do you know this tape is real?"

"Mr. Conklin, the FBI has been following me. They have killed two people to try to get this. They wanted me to lead them to this file, but I beat them at their game. I died. They think I died a week ago. I am actually officially dead."

"And, Tobias, just how did you die?"

"In an avalanche."

"Ah, yes," he said, raising his head looking at the ceiling, straightening his back, "on Mt. Washington."

"Yes, and sir, I need a copy of this. One for the Senate and one for the *Washington Post*. I am a journalist, you know."

"Yes, and a fine one at that. But, that would be two copies, wouldn't it?"

"No, sir, I don't want to keep a copy. I would prefer, as I remember you saying at that hotel, 'not to have my face fall off into my drink.'"

He laughed, holding his copious belly. "Abigail!"

The woman returned to the room. He told her he wanted Senator Richard Burr on the phone immediately, not in ten minutes, he wanted to talk to him now and, he boomed, "If his staff member says he is busy, you tell them I said this is a matter of national emergency. Interrupt him. And then when I have him on the phone, get me Martin Baron over at the *Washington Post*. Same story, no excuses."

"Richard Burr is a Republican, isn't he?"

"Young man, Richard Burr is one of the only men up on that Capitol Hill whose sense of human decency exceeds his sense of political necessity. Besides, he is my senator from the great state of North Carolina. I have faith that he is the man you need to talk to.

Now, while we wait for this phone to ring, tell me more of your tale."

I had just finished my story when the phone on the coffee table rang. He put it on speakerphone. J. William Conklin was clearly a good friend of Senator Burr. He told him I was at his table, listening in. He walked the senator through the whole story, as any thorough and careful attorney would. My God, I thought, this man is ponderous and slow. Can't he just cut to the chase? But the senator was equally ponderous in his questioning of Conklin. It became clear to me that these were two men who liked to get it right, particularly if someone else might die if they didn't.

"Mr. Starkey, I understand you wish to get this file to the *Post*. Can that wait until tomorrow morning? I need some time."

Here it was. Rule # 6 – *Never Put Your Finger on the Trigger Until You Are Ready to Shoot.*

"No, sir, I'm afraid I can't do that."

Conklin smiled. Gave me a thumbs up. A red button on the phone was blinking. The senator was silent, then, "Fine, I will send a car over to Attorney Conklin's office. There will be two Capitol Police Officers. You can give them the file."

"I am really sorry sir, but the FBI has been trying to kill me for a month. I can't trust that."

Again silence. "I will be there. You can hand it to me, can't you?"

"Absolutely, that is what John Hamilton would want. Thank you, sir." The line went dead.

Conklin pushed the red button. It was Martin Baron, executive editor of the *Post*. Conklin walked him through the same litany of events that he had laid out for Richard Burr. He advised him that he was on speaker phone and I was in the room.

"Mr. Starkey, what a dangerous adventure you have been on. Thank you for your bravery. It is exactly what makes the First Amendment so important. William said you work for *Globe*. Is that right?" Conklin had slipped a piece of paper in front of me. It said— *He used to be the editor of the Globe.*

"Yes, sir. I work for Sam Borstien."

He chuckled. "Why are you giving this to us and not to Sam?"

"Because if I go near the *Globe* offices, the FBI will arrest me or, they will realize I'm not dead, and kill me, then take the file. Mr. Baron, if I get this to you today, will you share publication with the *Globe*?"

"Of course. I will send a car to pick you up. I would like my editors to have you in the room as they prepare the story."

"Thank you, but I would only get in the car if you or Mr. Conklin were also in it." Conklin was shaking his head. "I guess it would have to be you, Mr. Boran."

"Ah, back to the Watergate days. I'll be there. Half an hour. William, thank you." That line also went dead.

"Abagail! Put everything away, lock the files and set the alarms. As soon as Mr. Starkey is safely ensconced in a fancy limousine, we are closed for business until this madness is over."

Two big black cars, both SUVs, arrived on the street in front of the law office at the same time. Two uniformed officers got out of each car, drew their weapons and held them two-handed at arms-length, sweeping up and down the street. An aide got out of each car, and after a brief talk with the officers, opened the back doors of the two vehicles. Senator Richard Burr got out of one and Executive Editor Martin Baron got out of the other. They shook hands, nodded sagely to each other and stepped into the alcove. I pulled my head out of the window, checked for my steno pad, took the two file

219

copies, hugged Abagail, shook Conklin's hand and bolted down the stairs. In the alcove, I handed a flash drive to each man.

"Again, thank you Mr. Starkey." The senator got in the back seat of his SUV and it drove off. I got into the other, Martin Baron got in and we headed to the *Washington Post*. It took a while. The driver went far away from angry crowds, almost into the suburbs, and then back into downtown. Boran was on the phone to his office, directing this and that—get it done, chop-chop.

The conference room was feted with food and drinks. There were three people in there when we arrived. A woman, probably in her fifties and two younger men. Each had a laptop. On the wall was a mega-screen. As soon as we walked in, Boran handed the file to the woman and she put it in her machine, typed furiously, hit buttons and the file appeared on all the laptops. The mega-screen lit up and there was Sam Borstien and two of the senior guys, skyped from his conference room. I knew the two by sight, but neither had ever said hello to me and no one had ever told me what their names were.

Sam Borstien said, "I'm real proud of you, Tobias, this is incredible work you've done."

"Thanks, say hi to Jasmine." I wasn't feeling real warm and fuzzy about him. 'Mr. Scoop-It.'

They all started in. Boran was in and out of the room. They knew what they were doing, they were professionals but none of them, except Boran, had ever done anything like this before. Not one of the men had even been born when Deep Throat lurked in the dark parking garage. They were using my story, as I'd written it, as their base. I liked that. The woman was really sharp. She kept asking me stuff like, 'You couldn't have known this, completely, until you knew that. Can I split them, swap parts?' Like that. Sharp. Focused. The

Boston folks were hanging in there, but it seemed they were a step slower.

They'd been at it for an hour and a half when the phone rang. One of the men answered it and handed it to Boran.

"It's Senator Burr." Boran took it. There were a lot of yeahs, nos and yeses, then 'I'll see'. He put his hand over the mouthpiece and said, "The senators do not want us to use the name of Richard Jimson. They say they have to advise both the Israelis and the British intel people first, they have to get their okay. If they don't, if we run it, it might compromise their operations and any chance we have of pursuing charges against the guy. What do you think?"

The woman said, "I think it means they're serious about going after Trump. Finally!"

The two men nodded. Then Boran looked at me. "Tobias, it's your story."

I was amazed he afforded me that level of respect. I sat a bit stunned. The sharp woman kicked my leg under the table and said, "A United States Senator is waiting for your answer."

"My answer is no. I want the name published. John Hamilton was very clear—find the curly-headed man, expose him and do not let them cover it up. I understand the issue of national security and protocol, but it is that issue that got us into this mess to begin with."

Boran nodded slowly, then told the senator, waited, then hung up.

"He said we might regret this."

"One more thing. Jimsonweed is noxious and poisonous. I want to call the whole damn thing, 'The Jimsonweed File.'"

The woman winked at me and whispered, "Perfect."

It was late Friday afternoon. The story would run on Saturday, the least read edition of most newspapers, but nothing to be done about that. They were not going to sit on it. The group was in the final edits. I told them there were four names I wanted kept out of print, confidential—Maggie James, Alice Turnbell, Ellen Pettigrew and Beanie Weeks.

Martin Boran had left the room. One of the two men had taken over. His name was Bob. Bob leveled his eyes at me.

"Confidential sources, those who remain anonymous, are only those people to whom you gave a guarantee of anonymity before they gave you information, or those who may suffer direct harm from the exposure of their names. Not people who you think would be happier if their names were not used. Do any of these people qualify for legitimate anonymity?"

"This is what I think. This file was the property of the FBI. These people aided me in the theft of that document. They could be charged with a crime."

"Fair enough for Turnbell and Ms. James but neither Ms. Pettigrew nor this Weeks kid did anything remotely related to the commission of a crime. Not from what I see in all your documentation. Nothing. That's where I am on it."

"If those are the rules, okay. But I don't like it."

"Hard part about journalism, Tobias, is that it's not for you, it's for everybody else. It doesn't matter what you like."

The woman said, "Jesus, Bob, what the fuck difference does it make? Why so hard?"

"It's going to make a big difference when we are in a federal court staring down the throat of an angry judge. Trump is not going to take this lying down. Okay, let's take out Turnbell and James and run this thing. All of it. Ship it."

"On second thought, keep Maggie's name in there. She'd be pissed if it wasn't. Dangerously pissed."

The woman walked me out, down the hall. We passed another conference room with the same set up I'd just walked out of—Boran standing up, directing. Three people at computers and the mega-screen running live takes on the riots.

"You might have to share your headline," she said.

"That's okay, but it's really one story, isn't it?"

She put her arm around my shoulder and gave it a squeeze. "You're a brave man, Tobias."

"Not so much. When you have to do something for a friend, you have to do it. Can you do me a favor?"

"Sure, anything."

"Could you call the Old South Ender in Boston. It's a bar. Tell them to buy lots of newspapers and tell them I'll be there at ten o'clock when they open. Now, how do I get to Union Station from here?"

"There is no possible way you can walk through that war. That's suicide. You can crash at my place. I have an extra room. Fly out tomorrow."

"I got a thing about seeing what Americans do. It's my country. In a weird way, we're all still one people just split in half at the hands of a madman. I want to see it. Oh, and I got a thing for the ticket lady on the red-eye to Boston. She is very cool. How do I get there?"

24

ON THE STREET, OUTSIDE THE BIG BUILDING, people were gathered, but they were dressed as though to go to work, not to battle. Their faces scowled or their mouths opened and their eyebrows raised, the voices low so as not to draw attention. They said things like, "Oh My God, what the fuck is happening?"

Three blocks from the *Post,* the crowds thickened. There seemed to be a pushing, a pulsing as one group, mid-street, got close to another knot of people, hurled shouts, threats and they threw things at each other, then pulled back away leaving empty asphalt between them—as though they didn't dare intertwine into body on body combat—yet. With each pulse, they got closer, louder, less restrained by any measure of judgement.

I couldn't stay separated from the crowds. I was sucked in. They moved, almost like herds of wildebeests on a run from a lion, a mass of bodies swinging together this way and that way until those bodies touched the bodies of another herd coming at them and their hoofs and horns clashed and dug into each other. Some carried signs and many signs were nailed below the top of the stick so the end could be sharpened and pointed, like a lance. Who told them to do that? Who gave them that idea? Somebody or something that wanted those sharpened points thrust into flesh.

One herd of wildebeests were white and mostly male. The other herd was darker-skinned and mostly female. It didn't seem like an even match until I got close into the eyes of the dark-skinned women. In there, was a ferocious red burn.

One of the men was clutching a child, a young curly-haired thing not more than four or five in a pink frilly dress. I saw a pointed stick gouge into the child's bare leg and heard the child scream into her daddy's face. The man had nowhere to go. He couldn't get out. He couldn't back up, he wouldn't go forward. He had signed up for this battle, brought his most beloved child with him and now he was stuck. He owned it—the whole, terrible thing. For me, at that moment, it all stopped, like video put on pause. I hoped that years later that man wouldn't show off her scar and proclaim it to be a wound the girl suffered in the early years of her valiant war on injustice. That wasn't what happened. Not at all.

I heard a shot, like a big firecracker, and a body fell. I saw a hole, a schism more like, open up where the crowd had parted around the fallen one. I dashed through and there was blood coming out of a hole in the neck. People were screaming. Where were the police? Where was the Army? Where was anybody who could stop this madness?

I ran again, through the schism, out the backside of the herd and down a mostly empty street. Ahead, near the National Mall, I could see a vast churning crowd of people moving closer and closer to the Washington Monument, the Lincoln Memorial, those beacons of courage, unity and liberty that we used to hold so dear. A cluster of policemen were gathered around a few squad cars on an empty street blocks away from any crowd.

"Um," I said, "what's going on out there. Why isn't somebody stopping all this?"

One of them said, "Can I see some ID?"

"Uh, sure." I gave him Bryce's driver's license.

He looked me up and down, then took my arm and spun me onto the trunk of his car. "Spread 'um!" He frisked me. Some others gathered around. A few didn't pay any attention at all. "He's clean." He handed me back my license. "I suggest you get your ass back to your ivory tower." I realized I still had on all my Harvard gear.

"Yes, sir. Which way is Union Station?"

He pointed. "Six blocks, turn left on Louisiana, four blocks up. Should be pretty quiet down those streets. You better hurry. The last train out of here going north leaves in, he checked his watch, forty-five minutes. Then we're shutting all stations down. No trains in means no trains out. Now beat it."

The streets were quiet until two blocks from the end. There was a group of youths milling around a store front. Eight or ten of them. One of them lifted a baseball bat and a window shattered. I ran to the other side of the street, but two more came from nowhere. I turned to run back and two more blocked me in. Looters, not protesters, not rioters, looters—the hyenas circling the outside of the kill. One shoved me hard. My face hit a parking meter as I went down on the sidewalk. A boot kicked me.

"Money. All your money, dude."

The tallest one yanked me up by my collar and shoved me against a plate glass window. A siren. Finally. But it sounded blocks away. I pulled my front pockets inside out—they were empty. I pulled my sleeves up, no watch. I reached into my back pocket and pulled out my wallet. That's as far as I got. He grabbed it and they ran. They must've netted three hundred bucks, plus Bryce's license and credit card. In my other back pocket was my passport and note pad. They didn't get that far.

The station was two blocks ahead. As I got closer, I saw people coming out. A train must have just gotten in, let them off and would now be loading for the final run north. I elbowed everyone as hard as I could and got to a ticket window. The guy was closing up, his cash drawer open, counting money. "Boston!" I shouted. He leaned over to the speaker hole.

"One way?"

Oh, thank God!

"Yes, sir, one way."

I bent down, took my shoe off and fetched my credit card and license out of my sock and put them both on the counter.

"Smart," he said, "credit card in your sock. Smart." He handed me my ticket. "Go through security, then track #11. You'll make it."

The police had cordoned off the entire entry to the platforms so that everyone was funneled through one make-shift metal detector. There was small area enclosed with a low chain-link fence. 'Throw All Signs In Here'. The pile was about two feet deep—*Fuck Trump, Send Them Back, Lock Her Up, Build the Wall, Babies Don't Belong In Cages.* A few of the spiked ends were red with blood. Even if the police were not going to get into the battles in the streets, they were also not going to allow them to occur on the trains, or, I guessed, busses, airplanes or ferry boats. That would not be civilized.

I sat back in my seat, an aisle seat, and touched my face. A great lump was growing above my eyebrow and it throbbed. It was probably going to turn purple, but I felt good. I felt like I had when I got to the top of Black Bear Hill—I did it! I did it! But there was no Mr. Hamilton to meet me at the bottom of this hill. He knew he wouldn't be here. That's why he had been so careful in his instruction—so that I would.

My ticket lady came. How sweet she was. She knelt down on a knee in the aisle and put her fingers soft on my forehead. "What's the other guy look like?"

"He got my three hundred bucks."

"You want a ginger ale, on me?"

"I would love that."

She walked to the back of the car, collecting tickets. She was back in a little while with a ginger ale, two aspirin and a damp cloth for my head.

"What time do we get into Boston?"

"Not 'till probably ten or so in the morning. This is going to be a long ride through the night. Each stop is going to take at least an hour, security and all. And we're going slower than usual."

"I guess the problem is all across the country."

"Honey, the problem *is* the country. There ain't nothing else anymore. How did this all happen?"

"Do you have a pencil?" She handed me one. I tore out a page of my note pad and wrote my name on it. "When we get to Boston, buy a newspaper. The answer will be there, on the front page."

She tussled my hair and walked away. She didn't believe me.

On and off through the night, I slept. This trip, I was awake in Penn Central. It was a madhouse at two o'clock in the morning. The station was full and people were still shouting. The pile of signs in the wire enclosure was huge and there were hundreds of cops. The car I was in was full. My ticket lady was about at the end of her rope. A guy in front of me stood up and started hollering about something and she put her hand flat on his chest and shoved him back in his seat.

229

"Now you sit down and shut up. For the whole damn trip. I hear one little peep out of your mouth, I'm going to throw your ass off my train—and then I'll call the cops. Now shut up!"

A big man near her stood up and said, "Hey girl, you need any help?"

She put her hands on her hips and said, "Do I look like I need help?" He sat down. She turned and pointed her finger at the guy she had shoved into his seat. "One peep, get it?" Maybe not quite at the end of her rope. Not yet.

Across the aisle from me was a young woman scrolling on her smartphone. Her blonde ponytail was pulled through the back-strap of a blue cap. On the front of the cap was, 'MAGA.' I told her I had never seen a MAGA hat in blue. She told me that it didn't stand for what I thought it stood for.

"What does it stand for?"

"Make America Good Again"

"Wow, how's anybody supposed to know that?"

She smiled. "Like anything else today. Spread the word and the word will be known. In the blink of an eye, the whole world will know what it means." She went back to her smartphone, thumbs blazing.

At eleven in the morning, I walked out of South Station into a warm December day. There was a newspaper kiosk on a corner. The headline of the *Boston Globe* was, **Donald Trump—A Russian Puppet.** Under that was, *Tobias Starkey – Globe Investigative Journalist.* I folded it into thirds and stuffed it into my back pocket, stuck a huge smile on my face and began walking the ten or so blocks back toward downtown, back toward Maggie and the Old South Ender.

HISTORICAL NOTE

While this book is a work of fiction, the foundation of the plot is based in fact. On November, 9, 1977, William Cornelius Sullivan was shot to death in Sugar Hill, New Hampshire. He had been the third highest ranking official in the FBI, in charge of counterintelligence and the notorious COINTEL Program. 1971, he had been fired by J. Edgar Hoover. Sullivan led the FBI team that investigated the assassination of JFK. He never turned over his secret files: not to his bureau, not to the Warren Commission, not to the Senate. He was scheduled, within a week, to give top secret testimony to the Senate Select Intelligence Committee on Assassinations. He never made it. His files have never been found.

His death was determined by the state Fish & Game Department to have been a hunting accident. A young man swore in a statement that, while hunting, he mistook Mr. Sullivan for a deer and shot him. He pleaded *nolo contendere* and the case was closed. Fish & Game and the NH State Police, refused to return the hunting rifle to the boy's father, a State Trooper, or turn over any documents pertaining to their investigations.

Six years ago, I began looking into the circumstances of this 'accidental death'. The New Hampshire Department of Justice, Office of the Attorney General was very helpful. The documents— depositions, reports, photos, logs and letters presented or referred to in this book are the documents supplied to me by the various state agencies pertaining to the death of William Sullivan. While I have fictionalized the circumstances of their presentation, their content is factual. In essence, I have transported the events of 1977 to the present.

ACKNOWLEDGEMENTS

My greatest gratitude is for the work of my editor and publisher, Tom Holbrook. He is there every step of the way. Tom knows books and he knows when a word, a passage, a scene doesn't add to a story.

This book would not have been written if my oldest brother, Peter, hadn't told me not to write it. While working for a newspaper in Boston, he had interviewed a very senior FBI agent whom J. Edgar Hoover hated and had fired. Peter came to my house in the woods of New Hampshire and wanted to hide out. The FBI was following him everywhere. That senior agent was later shot dead.

I asked my local police chief, Richard Conway, a smart and decent man, what he thought about it all. He said my problem wasn't the FBI, it was the CIA. Then he said, if I saw men in grey suits creeping around in the woods behind my house, not to call him.

I thank Jeff Goldberg and Harvey Yazijian for their thorough and insightful reporting for the *New Times*. They carefully presented facts and inconsistencies relating to an 'accidental death' that took place in New Hampshire in 1977.

John Conforti, an attorney with the New Hampshire Department of Justice, was invaluable to me. He worked with the Fish & Game and State Police departments to provide all information legally available to me concerning the same 'accidental death'. Neither department was inclined to comply with my request any more than they had with *The New York Times*. John was tough and fair. I got most of what I needed.

Special thanks to my son, Moses, for introducing a new word. The Trivial Pursuit question was, 'What is the shortest word in the English language using all the letters A,B,C,D,E and F'? He was washing dishes, far off in cannabis land. He stared in the sink a long, long time, then said, 'bedfaced'. I have set his word to type in this book.